Alvin Fernald, TV Anchorman

Alvin Fernald, TV Anchorman

Clifford B. Hicks

illustrations by Laura Hartman

Holt, Rinehart and Winston / *New York*

10 9 8 7 6 5 4 3 2 1

Library of Congress Cataloging in Publication Data
Hicks, Clifford B   Alvin Fernald, TV anchorman.
Summary: When Alvin takes a regular spot on a
news show, he helps solve an 11-year-old crime.
   [1. Television broadcasting of news—Fiction.
2. Journalism—Fiction.   3. Mystery and detective
   stories]   I. Hartman, Laura.   II. Title.
PZ7.H5316AKt   [Fic]   80-11415   ISBN 0-03-046521-4

*This book is for
the special kids in my life—
all of them.*

Contents

An Interview with Riverton's Most Famous Citizen

1 "Alvin, is it true the rest of the kids call you the 'Magnificent Brain'?" asked Don Brooks, the popular young TV newsman.

Alvin Fernald shifted his gaze from the beard in front of him to the lens of the TV camera, then back to the beard again. The beard sprawled across the face of the smiling young man seated across from him. *It looks a little lopsided*, thought Alvin.

"No," he said aloud. "The kids don't call *me* the 'Magnificent Brain.' They call my *brain* the 'Magnificent Brain.'"

"And why do they call it that?"

"Well. Well, I suppose because it's always getting me into trouble and then out again." Alvin, gazing across the brightly lighted TV studio, could see his sister and Shoie waving from behind the glass. He raised a finger and pointed. "And them, too."

"Who is 'them,' Alvin? The TV audience can't see who you mean."

"My best friend, Shoie. His real name is Wilfred Shoemaker. And the Pest. That's my sister. Her real name is Daphne, but lots of times I call her the Pest."

"Alvin, can you give me any examples of how your Magnificent Brain gets you in trouble?"

Alvin sat back in his chair and thought for a moment. He knew this was why he was being interviewed on the local evening news show. He was supposed to entertain the viewers—all the people of Riverton and the surrounding area who regularly tuned into Don Brooks to find out what was going on locally and elsewhere in the world. One of the most popular features of the show was the five minutes every night called the "Spotlight." Tonight the "Spotlight" was on Alvin Fernald.

And the spotlight should be me, thought Alvin. *After all, I'm the best-known kid in Riverton, probably the best-known kid in Marshall County.*

Alvin was a short, slim boy. Two things instantly impressed people about Alvin: his shock of orange hair and his inborn cockiness. The cockiness came from surviving countless harrowing adventures. Alvin Fernald knew that his biggest problem was to avoid being conceited, to avoid trying to live up to his reputation. As a matter of fact he *was* conceited, but most of the time he tried not to show it.

Now here he was, trying to appear like a good guy in front of the TV camera. He glanced again at the lens. His brain clicked. Actually, it wasn't the lens that both-

ered him. Behind that lens, he knew, were hundreds of thousands of people watching and waiting for him to prove that he *was* something out of the ordinary—or to fall flat on his face.

"Well, let's see," he began. "There was the time, when Daphne was five years old, that I put a gas engine on her tricycle. I'll admit I forgot to put brakes on it. She got going so fast down the Hickory Street hill that she couldn't stop. She sailed past the courthouse and crashed right through the door of Mr. McAllister's drugstore. Knocked down all his paperback books and a big display of diapers that was his special of the week. She hit the soda fountain just as Mr. McAllister was serving Debbie Flugel a double pineapple sundae. That's pineapple ice cream with pineapple syrup, you know." Alvin paused, thinking back. He grinned. "What a mess! Pineapple syrup all over those diapers!"

Don Brooks was grinning, too. "I imagine. Tell us about some of your other adventures, Alvin."

"Well, there was the time Shoie and I and the Pest found this tree that someone had cut the limbs off of, but the trunk and two big limbs were still standing. It was over by the Baptist Church. What was left of that tree sure looked like a huge slingshot.

"We went over to Pop Linkletter's garage and got some old truck inner tubes from him. We cut the tubes into long wide strips of rubber and tied them together, then tied the ends to the tree limbs.

"We'd seen this guy on television get shot out of a cannon the week before, and the Pest said she'd like to get shot out of a giant slingshot. Shoie and I put her in the slingshot, and hauled her back just as far as we could. Then all of a sudden we let go. She sailed up and over the tree just as nice and easy as the man shot out of a cannon. She flew right over the fence and onto the front lawn of the Baptist Church.

"There was a wedding that day, and the bride and groom were just walking out the door when the Pest slammed down into the grass right in front of them, along with the rice. The bride dropped her flowers and ran back in the church. I think they found her hiding in the choir loft. The Pest wasn't hurt much except for her knee and her shoulder and her left ear."

Don Brooks was smiling broadly, sharing his enjoyment with his TV audience. "How about one more adventure, Alvin."

"And then there was the April Fool's Day that Shoie and I and Snake-Hips Scott decided to play a trick on Miss Pinkney. She's the fifth-grade teacher, you know. We snuck up on her house after dark and . . . and . . . Well, the more I think about it the more I think I shouldn't tell that one, Mr. Brooks. It ended in a disaster, sort of."

"Do many of your adventures end in disaster, Alvin?"

"Well, I guess quite a few of them do. It's a funny thing, Mr. Brooks. I've noticed that people who are nervous try to avoid me. Sometimes people will even change over to the other side of the street when they see me coming. I wonder why this is."

"I wonder, Alvin." Don Brooks was enjoying himself. "Tell us about your hopes and dreams, Alvin. What new adventures do you have in mind? What would you like to do next?"

Alvin wiggled in his chair. Unconsciously he reached up with his right hand and tugged at his earlobe. It was a sure sign that the Magnificent Brain was slipping into gear. Alvin often imagined he could hear clicks and clacks, and even whistles and bells, inside the Brain.

After a long pause he said quietly, "I'm into anti-gravity machines right now. I'd like to build an anti-gravity machine based on opposing personalities. I've often heard it said that opposite things attract each other, and things that are alike push each other apart. I'm looking for a kid who is just like me—almost a twin. I'm going to stand him under my dad's stepladder, and I'm going to stand on the top step above his head. I have a feeling that if we both think hard enough about ourselves, and then if I give a little jump, maybe I'll sail on up into the air, who knows how high? That will be known as my Principle of Identical Personalities.

"Also I'm looking for a huge magnet. I want to bury it just under the grass in the yard. Then I'm going to get three or four kids and we're going to run across that spot carrying a manhole cover. If my calculations are correct, we'll suddenly shoot up into the sky." He paused, deep in thought. "I forgot about something. Maybe we'd get sucked down into the ground."

The cameraman was breaking up.

Alvin's eyes had glazed over. Daphne, who was fascinated with such things, had once told him that he was a victim of self-hypnosis every time the Magnificent Brain slipped into gear.

"Did you ever notice how clearly you can imagine a particular scene with your eyes closed? Like the Ferris wheel at the county fair, maybe, or your mother's hands holding a piece of cherry pie, or something good like that? Well, I have an idea for projecting thought waves through a Xerox machine, so you can imagine a picture, produce a print of it, and then show it to others.

"I believe that anything your mind can imagine, you

can achieve. That's sorta my life rule. Like, right now I'm feeding information into my Magnificent Brain on building the world's biggest yo-yo. I'll run it on Mom's clothesline, and drop it off the roof of the Fillmore Hotel, and—"

"All right, all right, Alvin. Enough! Enough! We've gone way over our time limit in tonight's 'Spotlight' already. I think we've seen some fine examples of your Magnificent Brain in action. Just one last question: What would you like to be when you grow up?"

Alvin considered the question for a moment. "I'd like to be *everything*. An inventor and a scientist, a farmer and a man who builds cars, a deep-sea diver and an astronaut. It would be much more fun being *everything* than just being *something*."

"How about a TV newscaster? Would you like to do that?"

"Yes, but not especially. I mean, it's not very hard to do and it can't be very exciting."

The cameraman burst into laughter, then quickly controlled himself. But there was no smile on Don Brooks' face. He said grimly, "Let me tell you, Alvin, that newscasting is *not* an easy job, and indeed it *is* exciting. Why do you say it's easy?"

"All you do is read from a piece of paper, or sit around and ask dumb questions."

Don Brooks glanced at the red eye of the camera, then toward the control room. His producer was seated there behind the glass, and could cut this off at any moment. He could switch to the weatherman waiting in

another part of the studio. Don Brooks glanced again at
the red eye of the camera, expecting it to wink out.
Instead it seemed to gleam even more brightly. Obviously the producer thought this was good entertain-
ment, and was determined to keep the "Spotlight" on
the tube.

"Why do you say the questions are dumb?" The
words came out stiffly, each coated with ice.

"Well, if I were in that chair interviewing a kid I'd try
to find out what *all* the kids of Riverton are doing, and
what they're thinking, and what their plans are, and
what kinds of tricks they use to fool their parents and
their teachers. Kids are pretty smart, you know. They
think about all kinds of things that grown-ups don't
even know about.

"You should get kids to reveal some of their secrets.
They make up a big part of Riverton, you know, but
nobody ever *listens* to them. Everybody *tells* them what
to do, but nobody *listens*. If you'd try listening sometime, you'd learn a lot. There's a man working in the
City Clerk's office who steals stamps and soap and
everything else he can lay his hands on. The taxpayers
should throw him out. And there are two men who are
supposed to be doing sewer work for the city, and instead they spend five hours a day playing pinochle in
Mickey's Tavern. Kids find out lots of things just because
there are so many of us. We're all over town, and we're
constantly moving around. We can't help but see lots of
things."

"All very interesting, Alvin. Maybe you should be

asking the questions instead of me." The newsman forced a self-conscious chuckle, and looked at the control room again. No help.

"Maybe," said Alvin.

Usually Don Brooks was the coolest and least nervous man imaginable. Right now he was embarrassed and his voice was shaking.

Suddenly he had an inspiration—how to get this kid off his back and, in a way, strike back at the producer who had cast him adrift.

"Alvin, if what you say is true, you must know almost everything that goes on in the Riverton schools. Why don't you *try* being a TV newsman? Here's my suggestion: a week from today, come back to the studio and take a shot at sitting in *my* chair. We'll give you five minutes to tell all the local school news. Five minutes. It will be interesting to see how you make out."

"Oh, I'll make out all right," said Alvin, realizing after he'd said it that it sounded cocky.

"You'll find out that it's a lot of hard work."

"Five minutes isn't very long. In five minutes I can't even tell you all the news from Roosevelt Grade School."

"Perhaps we'd better tape it ahead of time. Then if you decide you don't want it on the air, we can substitute something else. Do you *think* you can do it?"

"Anything my mind can imagine, I can do," said Alvin. "No need to tape ahead of time. I can just do it live."

Don Brooks shifted his eyes to the nearest camera and

started speaking in the rich voice that had brought Riverton residents their local news for the past five years.

"And there you have it, ladies and gentlemen. Tonight's 'Spotlight' has been focused on Alvin Fernald, often called the boy wonder of Riverton, accompanied by his Magnificent Brain. Next week at this time Mr. Fernald will present the news of Riverton schools. Right, Mr. Fernald?"

"Right. There's one more thing, Mr. Brooks. Did you know your beard is trimmed crooked? It's a little longer on the right side than the left—the right side as I'm looking at you, but of course that would be your left side as you're looking at me, and I—"

"And now—" the newscaster broke in quickly, "we go to Tony Baxter for the weather."

The camera's red light blinked out.

Alvin heard the newsman's long sigh of relief.

There was a shuffle in the studio, and the cameraman on the closest camera stepped forward, a big grin on his face. "You're a natural, son. You'll make one of the greatest TV personalities of all time. Before you know it you'll be interviewing presidents and prime ministers." He stuck out his hand. "My name is John Kubec. Mighty glad to meet you, Alvin."

Alvin stood up and shook hands. The man was about the same age as Alvin's father. He had the deepest brown eyes Alvin had ever seen—almost black—and they stared steadily at Alvin. The man's smile was open and friendly. Alvin had a sure feeling that this man was at home with himself.

"Good to meet you, Mr. Kubec."

"A friend of yours is a friend of mine, Alvin. Pete Hardin. He's talked about you a good many times."

"Yeah. He's in my grade at school. Good guy. I'll tell him I met you. Well, I better go now, Mr. Kubec."

Alvin, in turning to Don Brooks, had no way of knowing that he was turning his back on a man who would play a very big part in his life.

Help! Help!

2 "I know zilch about being a TV newsman," admitted Alvin, leading the way up the stairs to his room. "I shouldn't have been so cocky yesterday."

At the top of the stairs he casually stepped to one side and let the Pest take the lead. She was too clever for him, though. Stooping over, she pretended to tie her shoe, leaving Shoie to take the lead.

Shoie, a thoughtful look on his face, turned the knob and walked into Alvin's bedroom. At least he *started* in. The act of opening the door triggered Alvin's Foolproof Burglar Alarm. A boxing glove packed with stones, mounted on a short section of two-by-four, came whipping through the air. It was powered by a screen-door spring. At the last moment Shoie suddenly remembered the Burglar Alarm—he'd been caught by it countless times before—and tried to duck. He was too late. The boxing glove struck him smack on the nose, and he went reeling back into Alvin's arms, while a loud bell clanged and the lights in the room flashed on and off.

Daphne put her hand to her mouth and giggled. Her

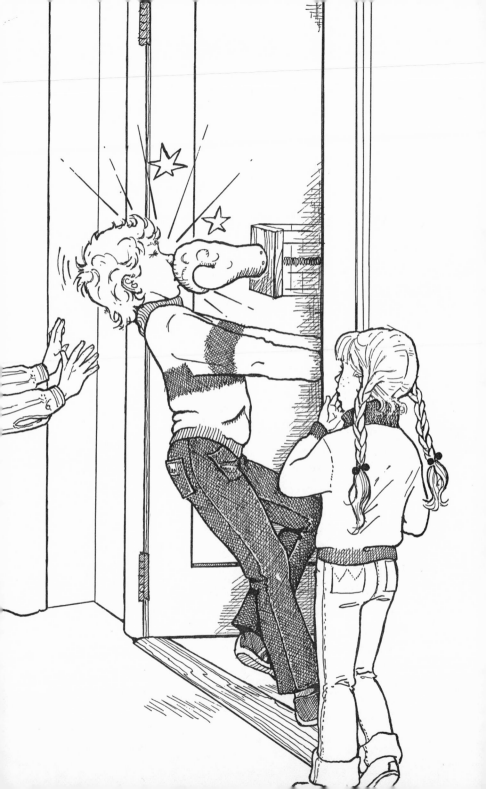

golden pigtails shook. "Shoie, I swear you'll *never* remember that dumb boxing glove that Alvin put up as a burglar alarm. I'll bet you've been hit by that thing fifty zillion times. Tomorrow you'll come up here and walk right into it again."

Shoie was staggering around the hallway holding his nose. It had instantaneously turned a brilliant red. "Oooowwwoooowww!" He moaned like a fire siren.

"Trouble with you, Shoie," Alvin said matter-of-factly, "is that you never wait for an invitation to come into my room. Now, will you please enter?"

Alvin pushed the boxing glove to one side, and led the way into the room.

The first thing he did, out of habit, was to unload his pockets, item by item, onto his Inventing Bench. Today he pulled out a rock that looked vaguely like an Indian arrowhead, an old flashlight battery, the last two bites of a peanut-butter sandwich, a tube of instant glue, a dead grasshopper, seven cents in change, a hard-boiled egg, and a small bottle containing Fire Chief McAllister's gallstones, preserved in alcohol after the Chief's operation and thoughtfully presented to Alvin as a gift from one old friend to another.

The Inventing Bench itself had achieved considerable fame, for it was here that Alvin had developed his One-Jerk Bedmaker, his Super-Secret Eavesdropper, his One-Shot Paper Slinger, and even his Automatic Man Trap.

After one of his particularly hair-raising adventures, Mr. Moser had written an editorial in the Riverton

Daily Bugle suggesting that Alvin donate his Inventing Bench to the Smithsonian Institution in Washington, D.C. Alvin had taken the editorial seriously, and had written the Smithsonian. Their framed reply was directly above the famous Bench. The letter thanked him politely for his offer, but said they simply had no room to display the bench.

Alvin Fernald could be many *kinds* of kids, and today he was no longer a Great Inventor. Today, for the first time in his life, he was a TV newscaster.

He dropped to his knees and looked at himself in the mirror Dad had mounted on the wall when Alvin was only three years old. Alvin had never bothered to raise it. He set his face in stern lines, tilted his head slightly to one side as Don Brooks did while he was on the air, squared his shoulders, and said in a loud, deep voice, "And that, ladies and gentlemen, is how the world looks to this reporter on Tuesday the 35th day of September." He thought that sounded rather distinguished. Shoie and Daphne, both sitting on his bed, roared.

"Oh, Alvin! If you only knew how funny you look down there on your knees, trying to be a big-shot announcer."

"Ho! Ho! Aarg!" Shoie was laughing and choking at the same time. "Our big TV man gives the news about the 35th of September. Alvin, Old Bean, there isn't any such date. The 35th of September! Aaarg!"

Alvin climbed to his feet. "Well," he said aggressively, "you just wait and see. You guys just wait and see! I'll be the best TV anchorman on the air."

" 'Anchorperson,' Alvin," said the Pest.

"What?"

"Anchorperson. Anchorperson. You know, Alvin. Women's Lib and all that. Everybody's a *person* these days."

Alvin walked over and sat on the stool in front of his bench. "Okay. I'll be the best anchorperson on TV." He paused a moment in thought. "Alvin Fernald, TV anchorperson. Has kind of a nice ring, doesn't it?"

Shoie kicked off his shoes and lay back on Alvin's bed. He was two inches taller than Alvin, and bigger all over, with a mop of yellow hair that stuck out every which way. He was the best athlete of Roosevelt School, and perhaps the best in the world. He and Alvin had been the closest of buddies as far back as either could remember.

"Alvin," he said, "why don't you give up the playacting, and decide what you're going to say on the air next week?"

"You're right, Shoie. We'd better do that. I'm including you in on this whole thing."

"Can I help, Alvin?" piped the Pest.

"I'll need all the help I can get." He picked up a pencil and a paper from his bench. "Okay, let's make a list of all the subjects I'll talk about on the air. What shall I put first?"

There was a long silence.

"What do you think I should talk about first?" repeated Alvin, looking straight at his sister.

"Maybe Miss Pilchard's ballet classes?" She said it in

a low, silky voice, as though offering the idea to him on a platter.

Shoie snorted. Alvin didn't bother to reply.

There was another long silence. Then, "What do you think, Old Bean?" Alvin and Shoie frequently called each other "Old Man" and "Old Bean."

"I think you'd better get the Magnificent Brain to work on this."

Alvin sat down on the floor with his back to the wall. The Magnificent Brain worked best when Alvin was comfortable. He closed his eyes, tugged on his right earlobe, and tried to think of a blank gray curtain. Nothing happened. No clicks or rattles in the Brain, no vision dancing brightly across the stage of his mind.

Alvin opened his eyes. "I'm getting nothing. Absolute zilch. This business of being a TV newsman is not nearly as easy as I thought it was. I think we need outside help."

"Outside help," mused the Pest. She often repeated his last words. "Outside help. I wonder who we could get."

"Maybe your parents," offered Shoie. "They're pretty smart. Or how about Miss Pinkney?" Miss Pinkney was Alvin's teacher.

"Nope," Alvin overruled him with authority. "You don't get the point of the whole thing. I said on the air that even a kid could do a good job as a newscaster. Now if I holler to adults for help, it will just prove that I was wrong. And I, Alvin Fernald—" he smiled, knowing they wouldn't take him seriously, "—I am never wrong."

"If we can't have adults help us, that doesn't leave us anything but kids," said Daphne with great logic.

"Okay. Let's figure out who'd be good at this kind of work. Who'd have ideas? Who could suggest interesting kids we could interview? Who knows what's going on in school—or after school?"

"How about Worm Wormley? He's pretty funny sometimes."

"We don't need anybody funny. We need somebody with ideas."

"How about Whispers Turner?"

"Naw. I saw him being mean to a cat once."

"How about Charlotte Kemp?" Shoie tried to toss out the name casually.

"Oh, come on, Old Man. Just because you like her better than any other girl at Roosevelt doesn't mean she's full of good ideas. Act your age!"

Another long pause. Suddenly there was a faint click. A shudder passed through the Magnificent Brain. Alvin blinked his eyes. He stood up, sliding his back straight up the wall.

"I've got it!" he said softly. "I know just the guy who can help us out."

"Just the guy," echoed the Pest. "Who?"

"Pete Hardin."

Silence, finally broken by Shoie. "Alvin, I think you're right."

"I do too, Alvin. He's got beautiful curly hair, and kinda dreamy eyes, and—"

"Be serious, Pest."

"I *am* serious."

"He gets the best grades of anybody in our class," offered Shoie.

"All the kids like him, so they'd tell him *anything* we want to find out about," said Alvin, his enthusiasm growing.

"He's full of ideas. Remember the play he wrote for Parent's Day? Remember the great April Fool's jokes he always plays?"

"Remember, too, that the cameraman at the TV studio is a friend of his. He's spent a lot of time around the studio, which would be a big help."

"And also remember," said the Pest with a far-off look in her eyes, "that he has the cutest little birthmark on his left shoulder."

"How do you know that?" asked Alvin suspiciously.

"He's on Roosevelt's basketball team," she replied sweetly. "And I watch every move he makes."

Plans for the First Program

3 "Of course I'll help you guys in any way I can."

Pete Hardin had a soft voice, but anything he said was spoken carefully after considerable thought. That's one thing Alvin liked about Pete. Pete didn't say a great deal, but when he spoke you knew it was the truth. Alvin recognized that he himself, in many ways, was just the opposite. He was inclined to blurt out his opinions without any thought, and he envied and respected Pete because he could control his tongue.

The four kids were lounging around the front porch of Pete Hardin's house. Alvin was lying on the old-time porch swing, his head propped up on one arm and his feet on the other.

"That's great," said Alvin. "I'll see that your name is shown in the credits."

"That's not important," said Pete, waving his hand. "What *is* important is that we all do a good job. I saw you on TV last night, Alvin. You were great. You've got to be even greater next week."

"Why?" asked Daphne, her eyes shining up at him.

"A lot of adults are down on kids for no good reason. They think we're goof-offs. We've got to show them that we can do a good job when we really try."

"What do you suggest, Pete? I mean, what shall we let me talk about?"

"First we need a well-balanced program. We—"

"Wait!" The Pest dug the stub of a pencil and a scrap of paper from one of her pockets. "I'll write down the ideas."

"We need a balanced program," repeated Pete. "For example, we need at least one big news story—a *real* news story that no one else has heard about."

"News story," repeated the Pest, writing.

"We need a top-notch feature about a kid—some kid who will be fascinating, not just to other kids, but also to adults."

"Top-notch feature."

"And for a change of pace we need a good sports story."

Shoie sat up. "I'll take that one. Sports. Maybe I don't have a Magnificent Brain like you, Alvin, but I know about sports. I'll come up with a good idea."

"To balance out the program, we need to expose some kind of scandal or corruption, and we need a commentary on some current news event."

"Fine," said Alvin. Then, "Pete, you're just the guy we need."

"And here's just the thing you need, too." The front door popped opened and a very short, rather stout lady walked out. She had short-cropped gray hair, and was wearing a red and white apron. She carried a large plate covered with a kitchen towel.

"Here's exactly what you need," she repeated, placing the dish on a small table. She lifted off the towel to reveal a mound of freshly baked cookies.

"I don't know whether you kids have ever met my Aunt Mildred," said Pete. He introduced each child in turn.

Aunt Mildred wore a warm smile that never seemed to leave her face. She joked with Alvin for a moment about his appearance the night before.

Alvin remembered, now, what Pete told him two or three years before. Pete was an orphan, and had been taken in by his aunt and uncle when he was an infant. He noticed that although Pete called the smiling woman Aunt Mildred, he treated her in the same casual, take-for-granted, but warm way that most kids treat their mothers.

The kids were polite until she disappeared into the house, then they pounced on the cookies.

"Where were we?" asked Alvin.

The Pest read her notes through the warm, buttery taste of a fresh sugar cookie. "News story. Feature story. Sports story. Scandal. Commentary."

Alvin Fernald
on the Air!

4 Alvin felt a trickle of sweat run down the back of his neck. He squirmed uncomfortably behind the gleaming modernistic desk. The lights came at him from every direction, and three cameras followed his every move.

He glanced up at the control room, directly in front of him and slightly above eye level. There was a slight reflection in the glass, but he still could see the News Director in the control room.

Clipped to Alvin's coat was a tiny microphone, and virtually buried inside his ear was a miniature speaker. As he looked at the Director, he could see the man's mouth form words.

"Fifteen seconds to go, Mr. Fernald."

The words seemed to come from right in the middle of the Magnificent Brain. They paralyzed Alvin.

Then the man was counting. "Ten seconds . . . nine . . . eight . . . seven . . . six . . . five . . . four . . . three . . . two . . . one!"

Alvin Fernald, long known as the cockiest boy in Riverton, almost fainted. For a long moment he couldn't manage to inhale. He gasped and promptly choked, coughing into the microphone.

"You're on! Say something!"

Alvin looked wildly about. Where was he? What was he doing here? What was he supposed to do next?

"Look at the teleprompter," hissed the voice in his ear.

Teleprompter? What was that? Oh, yes. Now he remembered. He peered at the area just below the camera lens. Letters swam across the area, and Alvin finally made out the words, "Good evening . . ."

Desperately Alvin pulled himself together, forced his brain to function, forced his eyes to focus, forced his tongue to wet his lips. His eyes left the teleprompter and searched for and found the red light on the camera.

He opened his mouth. "Good evening, ladies and gentle—" The words came out in a whispered squeak, barely audible.

Alvin closed his eyes, gulped a huge breath, and started again. "GOOD EVENING, LADIES AND GENTLEMEN, AND ALL YOU KIDS OUT THERE IN VIDEOLAND!!!!" This time his voice boomed forth with such volume that every audio dial in the control room leaped to the right and hung there, quivering.

"Not so loud," hissed the voice in his ear.

The trickle of sweat by now had rolled along the back of his neck and was moving down his back. It tickled. Alvin squirmed, rubbing his back against the chair.

Somebody giggled off to his left, behind the lights.

Alvin squared his shoulders and looked at the notes in front of him. He'd *be* an anchorman!

"I've been asked by Don Brooks to appear as a guest newscaster on this station. First I want to thank him on behalf of the kids of Riverton.

"And it's about time you recognized those kids. Maybe a third of the population of this town is kids, and who ever says anything about them? Kids do lots of neat things, and some things that aren't so neat, but who ever hears of them unless they get in trouble? Who knows what's really going on in the schools? The kids do. Who knows where school money is wasted? The kids do. Who knows when grown-ups cheat in grocery stores, or expeed the seed limit—I mean exceed the speed limit? The kids do." He leaned forward and looked squarely into the camera lens, as Pete Hardin had told him to do. "*Your* kids do.

"And now for the news . . .

"Flash! My investigators report that there is an absolutely secret entrance to Roosevelt School. When a kid enters fourth grade, he's sworn to secrecy and told about the secret entrance by a fifth-grader. Kids have known about it for maybe a zillion years.

"Not everybody uses the secret entrance, but a few kids do now and then. If you think about it, this explains why a few kids know exactly what grades they're going to get on their report cards. It explains how all those signs appeared overnight in Miss Trimble's room when it was her 25th anniversary as a teacher. And it also explains how two kids got into the school last year and vandalized it."

Alvin paused for a moment, gazed upward at the ceiling, then back at the camera. "You adults never caught the vandals, but we did. We caught them sneaking out of school. Our court system works fast, and it works fairly, which is more than you adults can say for your court system.

"Anyway, I wanted to let you know that there *is* a secret entrance to Roosevelt." He paused and smiled. "And I challenge you to find it.

"Flash Number Two, this one a social note. Miss Anne Dale, who teaches fifth grade at Warren G. Harding School, has been secretly engaged since last Saturday night to Phil Cope, the well-known young chiropractor. The happy event occurred on Miss Dale's front-porch swing at 9:27 p.m. The Junior Newsroom joins in congratulating the happy couple."

As he paused, the voice crackled through the microphone buried in his ear, "Cut it short, kid. Your time's about up!"

Alvin hurried on. "Flash Number Three! You adults ought to investigate the scandal in the high-school cafeteria. A company by the name of M & R Service holds the contract to provide food for the cafeteria. The owner of M & R Service is the brother-in-law of Al Perry, who runs the cafeteria. Because the food has been so lousy, some of my high-school friends have secretly checked on the cartons when they were delivered to the school. Supposedly full cans of spaghetti sauce are only half-full."

"Good Lord, Fernald! Be careful of what you're saying," warned the voice.

"I can prove every word of it," said Alvin in a vehement whisper, turning his head to one side in a desperate effort to talk to his ear.

"Half the cans delivered to the cafeteria are swollen because the contents have gone bad. A big slab of cheese marked '50 pounds' weighed only 35 pounds when it was delivered. Chunks of fat and gristle are buried in hamburger meat that is labeled 'prime.' " He paused. "I have a feeling there'll be some lights burning in the high-school cafeteria tonight. Maybe somebody from the school board should get over there right away, to prevent the evidence from being destroyed."

There was a rustle in the back of the studio.

"And while we're on the subject of the high-school cafeteria, here's a report on what the kids like to eat: Best of all they like hamburgers and hot dogs, with pizza as a salad and potato chips for dessert. Their least-favorite items are spinach, squash, and green beans with something called yuck on them. When my investigators asked what yuck was, nobody knew, but everybody just said 'yuck.' Better leave out the yuck from now on, Mr. High-School Chef."

Now there was a cadence of mirth in the background. The stagehands were making no pretense of suppressing their laughter. Through the bright lights, Alvin spotted Mr. Kubec standing alongside his camera with his hands on his hips and his head thrown back.

Alvin swung around, as Pete had instructed him to do, and faced another camera off to his left. "Now, short flashes from your news team, straight from the world of Riverton kids.

"A Fernald Flash! Cathy Kemp won the rope-skipping contest in Silvermont Park with a record 1,281 jumps without missing or stopping. This annual contest is sponsored by the kids of Riverton. Adults don't have anything to do with it, and that's the way it should be. Congratulations, Cathy!"

"Go ahead," said the voice in his ear. "Take all the time you want. You're doing terrific."

"Thanks," said Alvin out of the right side of his mouth, toward his right ear.

"A Fernald Flash! Jack Wetzel now has 18 garter snakes in his collection. Flash! The robin that lives on the balcony of the library had three babies last spring. All three grew up and have joined their mother and father in the long flight south for the winter. Flash! Hepzibah Stavisloscowicz will break the sex barrier and make the junior-high football team this year. We predict she'll make a fine quarterback. We also predict the cheerleaders will have trouble with her name."

"And now for my commentary." He lowered his voice to a know-it-all level. "It seems to this newscaster that the President's forthcoming trip to the Middle East is extremely ill-advised. The United States has nothing to gain and everything to lose in this latest round of talks.

"It is true that our energy shortage has reached the crisis stage, and we must look to Middle Eastern countries for increased shipments of oil.

"However, the President is going to these meetings hat in hand. Because of the disastrous weather this summer, we do not have a huge grain surplus as our chip on the bargaining table. And as my Uncle Louie says, you can't play poker without chips.

"This newscaster has a suggestion to make. Kids have a natural knack for getting along together. Oh, I know kids fight. Sometimes they even hurt each other. But when two strange kids meet they soon are playing together, and in some cases, within an hour they have made a friendship that lasts for life. Kids are natural peacemakers.

"Mr. President, why don't you invite a big delegation of kids from all the countries of the Middle East to come here for a visit. Let the parents come too, but it's the kids who are important. At the same time, Mr. President, send a batch of American kids over to those countries.

"Let the kids play together. They'll have a ball. And I don't mean play under adult supervision. Just let the grown-ups watch. Pretty soon, just by playing together, the kids will start learning each other's languages. And pretty soon it will dawn on the parents that kids are the key to peace."

Alvin let his eyes drop to the desk. He paused and took a breath. Then he looked up into the camera lens with a smile.

"And that's the way your Junior News Staff sees this 11th day of October. Over to you, Don Brooks."

A moment after he spoke those words the red light blinked out, and he heard Don say, "Good night, Ladies and Gentlemen. Now stay tuned for the IBS Evening News with Miles Sullivan."

John Kubec was the first to reach him. He vaulted across the desk and grabbed Alvin's hand, squeezing it as he pumped it up and down. "Alvin, you were great! Just terrific!"

The door to the room burst open, and in rushed Don Brooks and the News Director. Through another doorway came the producer, and Alvin could see the audio engineer waving from the control room. Three or four people reached him at once.

"Alvin, you were sensational!" said Don Brooks, putting an arm around Alvin's shoulder. "Sensational! To tell the truth, I thought last week that you were a conceited little rascal, and I could hardly wait to see you fall flat on your face right smack in front of the camera. I was wrong. I enjoyed every minute of your segment. Alvin, you're a natural newscaster."

"Good job, Old Bean," said Shoie's voice into his other ear. "A razzle-dazzle telecast."

"Razzle-dazzle telecast," echoed Daphne.

Pete Hardin was there too, standing beside Mr. Kubec, who had an arm draped casually around Pete's shoulder. "Well, you did it, Alvin," said Pete. "I guess it was worth all the work and rehearsals."

Alvin's chest was beginning to puff up. Words echoed through his Magnificent Brain. "Terrific." "Sensational." "A razzle-dazzle telecast." "Natural newscaster." Then his eyes swept the audience in front of him.

"I couldn't have done it without you guys—without you, Shoie, and you, Pest." He reached out and pulled gently on her pigtails. He looked across the desk at Pete. "And you most of all."

He stepped out from behind the desk and headed for the door. "C'mon, guys. I'm tired. On the way home I want to go past Roosevelt, and past the high school. I have a feeling there'll be lights in both those schools tonight."

As he headed through the lobby, he nodded at the blonde girl operating the switchboard. She was so busy she barely had time to nod back. Then he noticed the board in front of her. A zillion lights were flashing on and off, as though she'd earned ten free plays on a pinball game.

"What's going on?" asked Alvin.

"The town's gone crazy," she managed to say. "Everybody wants to talk about some kid named Alvin Bernard."

Alvin Becomes
an Anchorperson

 Alvin's mother picked up the phone. "Hello."

"Hello. Is Mr. Fernald there? Hrrmph. Mr. Alvin Fernald?"

"You mean my son Alvin? Nobody ever called him Mister before."

"Yes. Yes, that's who I mean. Mr. Alvin Fernald, the newscaster. Hrrmph."

Alvin's mother put down the phone. "Alvin, it's for you. Somebody who keeps saying 'hrrmph.'"

Alvin picked up the phone. "Hello."

"Hello. Mr. Alvin Fernald?"

"Yes, I'm Alvin."

"This is Lou Bessimer, General Manager of the TV station. Hrrmph."

"Hi, Mr. Bessimer."

"Alvin, you've got to come to work for us on a regular basis."

"What do you mean?"

"I mean that we're prepared to give you your own

five-minute segment of the evening news two days each week—Tuesday and Thursday."

"You want me to be a newscaster again, like last week?"

"Yes."

"Why?"

"Because you were *good*, Alvin. Hrmmph. Our phone lines have been jammed since your newscast. Everyone who saw you wants to see you again—and regularly. And everyone who *didn't* see you, now wants to. You're an overnight sensation, Alvin."

"I'll think about it, Mr. Bessimer."

"No! No! You must decide to do it, and *now*! Hrrmph."

"Let me think it over."

"I'll hang on."

Three seconds passed.

"I'll do it, Mr. Bessimer."

An audible sigh of relief. "Good. Good, my boy. You'll be paid, of course."

"Work that out with my folks. I'll probably either save the money for my college education, or buy some bicycle wheels for my next invention. It's my contribution to solving the energy problem. It will be sort of like a Chinese rickshaw but it will be pulled by trained—"

"I'll contact your parents later today. I'm glad we have a deal."

"Not so fast. I want your personal guarantee about some things."

"Hrrmph. What things?"

"First, I and my news team are the only ones who will decide what we put on the air."

A pause. "Well, now, Alvin, I assumed we might set up a regular review of each of your broadcasts before—"

"No. No review, or the deal is off."

"Well. Hrrmph. Well, all right."

"Second, you will assign a camera crew to us, whenever we want, to tape stuff that happens outside the studio. I think you guys call that a 'remote.'"

"Now, Alvin, that's much too expensive for kids to—"

"A remote camera crew or the deal is off."

"Well." A sigh. "All right, Alvin."

"And I want Mr. Kubec as the cameraman."

"But Mr. Kubec is our best cameraman and we save him for important—"

"Mr. Kubec. That *is* important."

"All right. You drive a hard bargain, Alvin."

"Third, I'll be having some kids help me, not just as a news team, but actually on the air."

"You mean you want *other* kids on the air with you?"

"Yep."

"This is getting much too expensive. We can't afford to pay them, Alvin."

"That's all right. I'll pay them out of whatever I make, Mr. Bessimer."

"Good. Then you can do it. Hrrmph. But be sure they behave themselves."

"Next, I want everybody to refer to me as Alvin Fernald, Anchorman."

Alvin felt a tug on his elbow. He looked down at the Pest, who had been listening to his end of the conversation. "Person, Alvin," she whispered emphatically. "Anchor*person*."

Alvin sighed. "You and Women's Lib," he hissed, his hand covering the phone. He removed his hand. "Better make that Anchorperson, Mr. Bessimer."

"Anchor what?"

"Anchorperson."

"We'll call you anything you like, Alvin."

"Well, I guess that's about all. We have a deal. But I'd like you to answer a question."

"Fire away."

"I don't think you hired me just because of a few phone calls. Tell me the real reason."

"Did you ever hear of a dollar, my boy?"

"Of course. Everybody has."

"Well, dollars are the real reason we want you on the evening news."

"I don't understand."

"That switchboard really did light up like a fireworks display. And our audience—the number of people who were watching—went up like a skyrocket. Whenever our audience grows bigger, we can charge more for each minute of commercial time we sell. So you can see why you are important to us, Alvin. Hrrmph. We hope—and expect—that you will build our audience on a regular basis. And that will mean more money to the station."

"I see."

"One other thing. We've been trying for years to sell commercial time to the Grandpa Clifford Company with no success."

"Yeah. I remember them. Grandpa Clifford's French-Fried Hamburgers."

"That's right. My wife and I eat those hamburgers

every Thursday night, regular as clockwork. Anyway, the phone rang today and believe it or not, it was Grandpa Clifford himself. He said, Alvin, that you remind him of himself when he was your age. You absolutely knocked the old geezer out. He said that with all the shabby shows on the air, your segment last night was the most refreshing thing he's ever seen on television. And he said he'd buy a full two minutes of air time to advertise Grandpa Clifford's French-Fried Hamburgers anytime we can get you back on the air. That's a lot of money, Alvin. A lot of money. Thousands and thousands of dollars."

"That makes me feel pretty important."

"You are, Alvin. Hrrmph."

"Okay, Mr. Bessimer. We have a deal. I'll see you next Tuesday night, ready to go."

"After what you did to the ratings for the evening news, Don Brooks is looking forward to working with you with a great deal of pleasure."

"He's a nice guy, even though I did make him mad when I said newscasting was an easy job." A pause. "Actually, it's not so easy. In fact it's pretty hard."

"Drop in and see me anytime, Alvin. I'll get in touch with your folks later."

"Okay, Mr. Bessimer. Thanks for calling."

"One more thing, Alvin. Powered by trained what?"

"Powered by trained *what* what?"

"You know. Your contribution to the energy shortage. A rickshaw powered by trained what?"

"Oh. Rabbits. They multiply like mad, so there'll be no shortage of power if we can just harness them to my rickshaws."

"Hrrmph. Well, goodbye, Alvin."

"Goodbye."

Alvin grabbed both of the Pest's pigtails and pulled them playfully straight out from her head. He looked down at her and whispered, "Alvin Fernald, Anchorman. Has a mighty nice ring to it. Hrrmph!"

Disasterville

6 The kids worked like demons all week, after school every day, and sometimes on into the evenings. By the end of the week even Daphne, with all her graceful energy, looked tired and wilted.

Alvin kept their spirits up, but it was Pete Hardin who took command. He insisted that they gather every scrap of information on a story they planned to cover, and if he thought they had missed anything he promptly made them retrace their steps to get it. He was the iron man of the crew, and his hand was the ruling hand.

Three days before their second program, Alvin decided to make a test. He conferred with his Magnificent Brain, which pointed out how valuable he was to the station. He lifted the phone, stuck out his chest, and called Mr. Bessimer's number.

"We need a remote crew right after school," he said crisply.

"Sorry, Alvin. Nobody's available."

"Mr. Bessimer, we had a deal. Shall we call it off?"

After a long pause, Mr. Bessimer cleared his throat.

"Hrrmph. Okay, Alvin. You win. I'll have a crew for you at four this afternoon. Where do you want them?"

"Oostermeyer's farm. It's out on West Main Street."

"For heaven's sake, Alvin! There's nothing on a farm that has anything to do with the kids of Riverton."

"That's where you're wrong, Mr. Bessimer. Dead wrong. And be sure you send Mr. Kubec." He hung up.

The more he worked with Mr. Kubec, the more Alvin liked him. He was a soft-spoken man, quiet and almost shy in everything he did. Except for his laugh. When he laughed it boomed out like a foghorn, and his whole face took on a strange radiance.

It was obvious that Mr. Kubec enjoyed working with the kids, and indeed he taught them a great deal. On their first "remote" at Oostermeyer's farm he quietly suggested different camera angles, novel lighting effects, and questions to ask that never would have occurred to any of the kids. In their story conferences he pledged himself to secrecy, and entered into their small conspiracies. Both Alvin and Peter were determined to keep their stories fresh, unseen by anyone at the station until they actually went on the air. And Mr. Kubec emphatically agreed.

On Monday evening Mr. Kubec arranged for them to have a special studio available, equipped with tape monitors, for a final rehearsal. He himself played the tapes they had taken so none of the engineers would see them.

It was a disaster.

By the end of the rehearsal Daphne was in tears,

Shoie sneaked out of the studio, and Alvin watched his own morale crumble into dust. He stuttered when he talked, forgot his cues, and left out one entire story. When a remote they had taped at Roosevelt School came on the monitor as scheduled, Alvin inexplicably went into a commentary that had absolutely nothing to do with what he was watching on the face of the tube.

It was such an overwhelming mess that Alvin finally suggested they resign.

"Not on your life," said Pete emphatically.

Mr. Kubec nodded his approval.

"We're all tired," said Pete. "Let's get some sleep. Tonight was disasterville, but I know we'll do a good job tomorrow night. I just *know* it."

"Come on, kids," said Mr. Kubec in his quiet voice. "I'll treat you all to one of Grandpa Clifford's hamburgers. Then go home and forget about the program."

They all climbed into Mr. Kubec's aging car and headed for the drive-in. But Alvin was worried. So worried he ate scarcely half his hamburger.

"Over to You, Alvin Fernald"

7 "Starting tonight," said Don Brooks, looking into the camera, "we are expanding our Riverton area coverage of the Evening News. Every Tuesday and Thursday we will explore in depth a sector of our society that is not normally represented in our news coverage."

He was seated at his newscaster's desk, handsome, relaxed. There was an earnest look on his face—an expression that had settled there like a mask as soon as the red camera light winked on.

In a far corner, the stage crew had built a set for Alvin. It was simple, and quite small. The backdrop was bright yellow. Alvin was seated at a desk exactly like the one he had at school. (Mr. Kubec had suggested this, rather than a glittering modernistic slab.) A few inches below Alvin's chin dangled a miniature microphone, suspended by a cord around his neck.

Daphne, Shoie, and Peter were waiting in the wings.

"Yes, we are expanding our news coverage," Don

Brooks said crisply into his microphone, "to include seg-
ments on the *children* in our broadcast area. There is a
special subculture out there that too many of us adults
know little about.

"To guide us through this subculture twice a week we
have selected a well-known young man from Riverton.
His name is Alvin Fernald. We have reported in the past
on some of Mr. Fernald's escapades—I mean adventures." Don Brooks gave a quick smile. "And now, for
his first regular newscast, here is Alvin Fernald, TV Anchorperson."

"You're on, Alvin," the Director's voice whispered
into Alvin's ear.

The red light on the camera directly in front of Alvin—Mr. Kubec's camera—winked on.

Once again, Alvin Fernald was petrified. He'd
thought it would be easy this time—after all, he'd done it
once before. Alvin opened his mouth, and nothing came
out, so he closed it again. He cleared his throat. The
little red light hypnotized him. He couldn't even blink
his eyes.

The silence seemed to stretch for an hour. Off to the
side—too far to the side to be seen—the other kids waved
their arms frantically.

Alvin opened his mouth once more, and still no words
came out.

Then, directly in front of him, despite the glare of the
studio lights, Alvin saw a movement. Mr. Kubec had
stepped out from behind his camera and was standing
beside it. He stared long and hard at Alvin.

That look gave Alvin the confidence he needed. He glanced down at the papers in front of him, then looked back up at the camera. He put on his "sincere" face— the face he had practiced in front of his mirror for hours—and began speaking rapidly.

"Our lead story on tonight's edition of the Junior News involves two boys from Chicago, 12 and 13 years old, who were arrested by Riverton police night before last inside the Buy-Good Supermarket. A rear window of the market had been broken. The boys now are being held on charges of breaking and entering, burglary, and theft.

"The breaking and entering consisted of one broken pane of glass. The burglary and theft, for your information, consisted of two pieces of salami the boys were eating at the time they were arrested. Nothing else inside the store had been disturbed.

"Your Junior News investigators talked to the two boys. According to their story, they are orphans who grew up in the same foster home in Chicago. They say they have been physically abused for years by the man in charge of that home. The younger boy showed us bruises and scars on his back, stomach, and legs.

"They further said that because of this mistreatment they had run away from the foster home, and were on their way to North Carolina to visit an aunt of the older boy. They had no money. They were hungry. They broke into the Buy-Good and ate some salami.

"By asking around, we found kids in Riverton who had cousins in Chicago. We called the cousins. They investigated for us. Now we know that every word the boys say is true.

"If those boys are guilty of a crime, then *every adult who permitted that crime to take place is guilty of an even bigger crime.*"

Pause. "And now for an update on last week's story about the high-school cafeteria."

Alvin knew he had been speaking too rapidly, but somehow he couldn't slow down. Then once again he noticed a movement in front of him. Mr. Kubec was making a long stretching motion with his hands. It was a signal that Alvin had learned well during their rehearsals. Stretch it. Go slower. Make it last longer.

For the first time, Alvin smiled into the camera. He relaxed. Still talking about the high-school cafeteria, he pivoted off his chair, stood up, walked around to the front of his desk, and casually sat down on it.

Alvin Fernald, Anchorperson, was in total control.

". . . Now that the cheating at the high-school cafeteria has been cleaned up by the police, the kids there tell the Junior News that they're getting much better food than they've had in years. Lolly Higgin even stated that for the first time in her life she tasted the yucky creamed peas and liked them. That's going a little too far for your Anchorperson, though."

Alvin paused deliberately, looking down at the paper in his hand. Then he looked up again, smiling. "Now we bring you a special feature of our Junior News coverage—the Junior Sports News. And here is your sportscaster, Shoie Shoemaker."

Shoie, the Greatest Athlete of Roosevelt School, sidled onto the set. He had the biggest feet of any 12-year-old in the county, and probably in the state. Right now those feet were inside an enormous pair of Adidas shoes, and just as he approached Alvin's desk, within camera range, the toe of his left shoe snagged a loop of electric cable running to one of the lights. Shoie's head came down and he pitched straight forward, as though he were the lead blocker for an off-tackle play that was bound to go for a touchdown.

Shoie ended up across Alvin's lap.

Alvin instantly started laughing.

Shoie scrambled to his feet and sat down at the desk. His face was bright red. He turned his head and glanced sideways at Alvin.

At that point Shoie's big chest heaved, and then he too was laughing. He reached down and picked up his notes, which were scattered across the floor. He put on his serious face.

"Sports Flash! Last Friday the Blue and Gold Anteaters of Warren G. Harding Grade School beat the Octopuses of James A. Garfield School 67 to 3 in a game of touch football. It was a hotly congested game all the way until late in the fourth quarter, when all but two of the Garfield kids had to go home for a Cub Scout meeting.

"Sports Flash! In an amazing display of athletic powress—" Shoie turned his head sideways and said, "Hey, Pete, is that word 'powress' or 'prowess'? Well, anyway, all you guys who are watching me on TV, Alice

Wetzel kicked a long one in the Tigresses' last kickball game. The gym floor had just been waxed and Alice slipped as she rounded third base. She slud all the way to the plate with the winning run.

"And now, by videotape, we bring you a Junior Sports Special Feature. We take you to Wilma Oostermeyer's farm for the annual Pig-Riding Rodeo. Most of you adults who are watching probably never heard of the Pig-Riding Rodeo that the kids hereabouts have each year. That's because we want it to be just our own event, without any adult supervision. So for years we've snuck out to Oostermeyer's and rode the pigs."

To Alvin's left was a TV monitor. As Alvin watched, Shoie's face dissolved and the remote tape came on. The camera focused on a crude sign that read "Tenth Annual Pig-Riding Rodeo." It then panned left to a pen. Kids of all ages were hanging from the surrounding fence.

"First out of the chute will come John Linkletter riding a pig called Son-of-a-Gun." The camera spun around toward a gate at the far end. Suddenly the gate swung open. Out came a half-grown pig with little Johnny Linkletter on its back, legs clasped around its belly, arms flailing wildly for balance.

"Ride 'im, Johnny boy!" shouted Shoie, totally excited by this scene of athletic "powress." He had forgotten his sportscasting job. Alvin gouged him in the side with his elbow.

Shoie described the rides of two other kids, and then said, "And here comes the winning ride, by Paul 'Hotpants' Irving, riding Screwtail." Once again the gate swung open. This time a kid no more than six years old was perched on a particularly huge pig's back. He had an almost magical sense of balance. The pig raced all the way around the pen, desperately trying to dislodge him.

"Now watch this, you guys!" shouted Shoie, getting excited again. At one moment the pig was racing like the wind. The next moment it spread all four feet and came to an instant stop. Little Hotpants went flying over the pig's head, did a complete somersault in mid-air, and landed on his belly.

"Oooooooofffff!" said Sportscaster Shoie. "That one hurt. Now watch."

The pig made a circuit of the pen, trotting slowly, then spotted the boy spread-eagled on the ground. The animal instantly shifted into high gear, lowered its snout, and ran straight for Hotpants.

There was a gasp from everybody in the studio.

Suddenly a lithe figure dropped from atop the fence. A long mane of silky black hair trailed behind the little girl as she ran toward the pig. In her hand she carried a bright red sweater.

"I tell you, she's gonna win the race to Bobby! See there? What did I tell you? Now she's waving that red sweater. And there goes the pig. Watch it now. Here comes the pig again, and again. The pig's gettin' kinda pooped. And there goes Little Hotpants, staggering over to the fence."

The monitor tube ceased glowing. Now it was the red bulb on Mr. Kubec's camera that was aglow.

"That girl's name is Giggles Malone. Hotpants won the prize for the longest ride, but Giggles won a special prize we awarded her on the spot.

"Saturday night Giggles and Hotpants were seen carving a punkin together on Giggles' back porch, and your Junior Sports reporters since have learned that Hotpants will take Giggles to the Roosevelt Halloween Party."

Suddenly Shoie smiled at the camera. "That last part ain't exactly sports news, but we thought you'd like to know. And now, back to our Anchorman. Over to you, Alvin."

"Thanks, Shoie. Now we present another regular feature of our telecast, the Junior News Weather. Here's that pretty little forecasting lady, the Pest—ooooops, I mean Daphne."

She skipped gracefully in from the wings. In honor of the occasion she had rebraided her two pigtails, which danced like a shower of gold around her head. She was wearing her best pair of jeans, and a new pair of sneakers she had persuaded her mother to buy her that morning. There was a big smile on her face, and the brightly lighted studio seemed to glow even brighter as she looked radiantly into the camera.

"Hi, out there. You may think that I can't forecast the weather very good, but I can. I've got some secret weather instruments that are even better than Mr. Baxter's instruments. Incidentally, I like Mr. Baxter real well. I think he's cute. Don't you think so too?"

Someone in the studio laughed.

"Anyway, one of my secret instruments is my Uncle Bienfang. Let me think. He's my mother's uncle by a second marriage. Don't you think that's interesting? I'll bet you do. Anyway, Uncle Bienfang lives on a farm out in Iowa, and when we visited him he let me ride on the tractor and jump in the hay. I guess that doesn't have much to do with weather forecasting. In a way it does, though. Because everybody in central Iowa knows that Uncle Bienfang is the world's greatest long-range weather predictor.

"This morning I called Uncle Bienfang. It was a long-distance call, but the television station paid for it. Don't you think that was nice of them? I suppose they paid for it because it's their weather. I don't mean it's *really* their weather, because it's *everybody's* weather. But any of Uncle Bienfang's predictions that go on TV are theirs. I think you know what I mean.

"Anyway, Uncle Bienfang sure was surprised to get a long-distance call from me. He's just beginning to pick corn out there, so he's pretty busy. He says his second wife—that would be my new aunt-in-law, I guess—Alvin's aunt-in-law too—was making lots of apple butter.

"I asked Uncle Bienfang for his long-range forecast. He said that just last week he had dug up some corn roots—that's one of the ways he tells how cold the winter will be. He also checked three almanacs that he had, and he got close enough to see the mother skunk that lives under his old corncrib. He can tell about the weather by how long the fur is on the skunk.

"Anyway, here is the Junior News long-range

weather forecast, based on stuff that Uncle Bienfang told me. It's going to be fun for the kids with sleds this winter because we'll get more snow than any winter since 1964. I can't remember that far back. Probably because I'm not that old.

"Also, the skunk's fur says it will be a very cold and windy winter. So that's what we have to look forward to. Let's all try to keep our spirits up in spite of it. Think of the poor Eskimos.

"Now I'm going to tell you my weather forecast for *tomorrow*. I have a different instrument for that."

Daphne had never liked the ballet lessons that Dad had insisted she take, but they had made her lean little body as agile as a willow branch. Abruptly she brought her left foot up and onto Alvin's desk. With the camera recording every movement, she jerked the shoelace, then pulled off the sneaker.

She wiggled her bare toes. "Ahhhhhh! That feels good. I've always thought that anything is better with your shoes off, except maybe hot asphalt.

"Mr. Kubec, will you please point your camera right at my bare foot? Yes, that's right. Thanks. I can see my foot on the monitor now. Funny feeling. Makes me feel like I have three feet and fifteen toes." She giggled.

"Now take a good look at that big toe. I'll bet you're saying it doesn't look like anything special. Well, it's a much better weather forecaster than any of Mr. Baxter's instruments. I broke that little toe playing kick-the-can when I was five years old. After it got well I began to notice that it was funny. I mean, it would tell me what

the weather would be like the next day. Like, if it doesn't have any feeling at all it's going to be a nice warm day. If it's going to be cloudy and maybe drizzly, it aches real bad. Eating a cookie helps. And if it aches bad and kind of curls down at the same time, it's going to be rainy, cold, and windy.

"Just a little while ago on this newscast, Mr. Baxter said that tomorrow would be cloudy and cold, with showers likely in the afternoon. He's a cute man, but he's wrong about tomorrow's weather. Tomorrow will be clear and warm for October—a high of about 58 degrees.

"I can't give you the outlook for the next day because my weather toe doesn't work that far ahead.

"Now back to our Anchorperson, Alvin Fernald!"

Alvin instantly looked up at the camera. He plastered a big smile across his face. "That's it, folks! That's the way your Junior News Staff sees this 27th day of October.

"Over to you, Don Brooks!"

Aftermath

8 The Junior News was supposed to last five minutes, with one break for commercials. Instead, the kids had been on the air more than eight minutes.

No one was complaining though—at least not yet. Everyone hung around to see what the audience reaction would be.

Don Brooks, as soon as he signed off, rushed over to Alvin and slammed him on the back. "Oooops! Sorry, Alvin! I just wanted to let you know how great you were."

"I was pretty good, all right," admitted Alvin modestly. "But the Pest talks too fast and too much. And Shoie doesn't read his lines too good. Maybe we should do more rehearsing next time." He punched Shoie on the arm; it was an old signal between the two that the speaker was really kidding—that he didn't mean what he'd just said.

To the astonishment of everyone in the studio, Shoie did a standing back flip and ended up on Alvin's desk. He looked down and said, "Hi, Mr. Kubec! Do you think we did okay?"

Mr. Kubec was standing beside his camera. "Great! Don't you think so, Pete?"

Pete's face normally showed very little emotion; now his eyes were shining. "I think we did very well," he said. "And I have some ideas for improving the Junior News. We'll start working on them right away. Alvin, I think that during the opening shot, you should—"

"Whoa! Not so fast, Pete," said Mr. Kubec, looking down at the boy with a smile. "You kids have worked mighty hard the past few days. Now's the time to relax. Pete, just before we went on the air your aunt called and invited the Junior News Staff over for popcorn and apples after the show."

"Let's go," said Pete.

The kids were putting on their jackets when Mr. Bessimer, the station manager, rushed into the studio.

"What a show!" he shouted, waving a wad of papers. "The switchboard is jammed. People are calling from as far away as Kingston and Liverwort. A messenger just hand-delivered this envelope. It's a long-term contract from Happy Frankenheimer. You know, 'The World's Greatest Wheeler-Dealer in Bicycles; when we make a deal you ride out *HAPPY!*' Happy is buying a thirty-second spot every time the Junior News is on the air. We've never had such a response to a program in the history of the station." He was so excited that his eyes were bugging out. *He looks a little like that pet frog I had last year*, thought Alvin.

"Sorry we have to leave, but we have a date with a bowl of popcorn," said Mr. Kubec.

As Daphne was heading toward the studio door with the other kids, she saw Mr. Baxter rolling up his fancy weather map. Their eyes met. He walked over to her.

"Don't forget to wear your raincoat to school tomorrow," he said with a smile.

"I won't need it. Betcha an ice-cream cone that it doesn't rain a drop tomorrow."

"I'll take that bet."

The next day was one of the sparkling clear days of Indian summer. There wasn't a cloud in the sky. And the temperature reached 58 degrees.

The Junior News Makes TV History

 9 The golden days of fall fell one by one, like the leaves of the trees, for Alvin and his TV staff. Schoolwork came first, insisted all the parents, so the kids were more eager to do their homework—to get it out of the way—than they ever had been in their lives.

Each day, at the earliest possible moment, they plunged into their TV work. Pete was a constant source of ideas. He had become the most important person involved in the telecasts, more important than Alvin. Yet Pete never was seen on camera.

Because Pete's role was so important, the kids instinctively began holding staff meetings and rehearsals at his home.

Whenever the planning sessions were held in the evenings, Mr. Kubec joined them. He would sit in an easy chair in one corner of the living room, eyes half closed, listening to the kids. Occasionally he would offer a suggestion in his slow, soft voice; it was a good one.

One evening as the meeting was breaking up he said,

"You kids don't need me anymore. It's your program. You should plan it yourselves. I'm bowing out."

Alvin was appalled. "We *can't* get along without you. You've *got* to stay."

"You come up with more ideas than all the rest of us put together," chimed in Pete.

"More ideas," echoed the Pest.

"Isn't the program any fun for you?" asked Shoie, a hurt note in his voice.

"Of course it's fun," Mr. Kubec replied hastily. "I really enjoy working with you kids. But it's *your* program. *You* should do it."

"I was wrong, once in my life," said Alvin seriously. "That was when I insisted we could handle the newscast without any help from adults. We *do* need you."

Mr. Kubec smiled. It was a smile of warmth and satisfaction. "Well . . . Well, okay. I'll stick around for a few more weeks. But mainly I'll watch, and help only when you ask."

Alvin had the feeling that Mr. Kubec was secretly relieved they had talked him into staying.

With each program the fame of the Junior News soared. Calls and letters poured into the station. Local advertisers were clamoring for spots. Mr. Bessimer obviously knew a good thing when he saw it, and began broadcasting spot announcements day and night, reminding viewers, "Watch our crazy kids; they're broadcasting the Junior News, but they're making television history."

Mr. Moser did another story on the Junior News for

the Riverton *Daily Bugle*; the big newspaper in the state capital sent a reporter and photographer for a feature article. Six weeks after the broadcasts began, two pages of pictures of the Junior News Staff appeared in *Famous People* magazine (it followed a one-page story on Hollywood's most beautiful starlet, noted Alvin; in fact his copy of the magazine automatically opened to the article about her instead of the kids!).

Best of all, they *were* making television history. They were pioneers, said Mr. Kubec. They had the first television show planned, written, and broadcast by kids.

Strange things began happening around Riverton. Very few people were on the streets between 6:00 and 6:30 Tuesday and Thursday evenings; the downtown stores might as well have closed their doors because there were no customers. Church socials and lodge dinners were postponed from 6:00 until 6:45. Ice-cream sales went down, while beer consumption went up; there were TV sets in the taverns.

Alvin had frequently been the center of attention because of his past escapades, so he wore the mantle of fame easily across his shoulders. Not so Daphne and Shoie; they became instant celebrities.

On their way home from school, other kids performed daring and sometimes disastrous athletic feats in front of Shoie. They even tried to buy their way into the Junior Sports news.

So many kids wanted to rub Daphne's weather toe— all her socks suddenly had holes in them—that she considered charging a penny per rub; she had to do *something* to bring in some money.

The Owls of the Network

10 The Riverton TV station is part of the International Broadcasting System (known as IBS). The symbol of IBS, shown every half hour night and day, is an owl with enormous eyes looking straight at the viewer. An owly voice says "Whoooooo?" answered a moment later by another voice saying "Everybody, that's whooo! Everybody watches IBS!"

It was inevitable that the *real* owls of IBS—a handful of New York broadcast executives—would, through their own pipelines, hear about Alvin Fernald, Anchorman, and his Junior News Staff. And it is the big owls who make the big decisions in TV programming.

The first hint that the owls were gazing toward Riverton came in a routine-looking request for the station to provide New York headquarters with a tape of the latest Junior News program. Virtually all live programs on TV are taped in case they are to be rebroadcast, or in case a lawsuit should develop over something said on the program. The request for the tape was routine except that it was addressed *personally* to Mr. Bessimer, who ordinarily would not have been involved.

At that moment Mr. Bessimer was basking in the un-
expected and incredible success of the Junior News. Advertisers were begging for 30-second spots, money was
rolling in, and ratings were soaring. Mr Bessimer
dreamed of a big bonus for himself at the end of the
year. Therefore his first thought when he received the
request for the tape was to run wildly through the station, shouting about this latest development. Still, he
didn't know exactly *why* New York wanted the tape.
Better take it easy, he cautioned himself. He mentioned
the request only to the station's Technical Director, who
provided him with the tape.

The anchorman for the entire IBS network news operation was Miles Sullivan. Because of his constant ex-
posure on TV, Miles Sullivan's face was better known
than that of the President of the United States. He was
boss of thousands of television reporters, cameramen,
directors, video engineers, audio engineers, and technical advisers scattered throughout the country. Millions
of people throughout the nation—actually throughout
the world—sat down each evening and flipped on their
TV sets, turned them to the local IBS station, and sat
back to learn what had happened in the rest of the
world throughout the day and what Miles Sullivan
thought of it.

On the air, Miles Sullivan had a constant, serious,
"the-world-is-doomed" look. One newspaper cartoonist
frequently depicted him with the eternally sad face of a
basset hound. On the air he gave the impression that he
was a person somehow set atop a mountain to view the

world from a vantage point no other human being could possibly command.

On the air or in print, no one ever referred to Miles Sullivan by just his first name or just his last name. He was always Miles Sullivan.

It therefore would have come as a huge surprise to his millions of viewers to learn that Miles Sullivan had a wacky sense of humor. Among his very small circle of close friends he was called Mickey. He was a man who played wild practical jokes on them. He dressed as a clown for their children's birthday parties. He was beloved as a warm and gentle person—the exact opposite of the personality he showed on the air.

This particular November afternoon, Miles Sullivan was in his office on the 58th floor of a New York skyscraper. He was standing at a window watching as the first few snowflakes of the year found their erratic way down toward 52nd Street far below. Weatherwise it was a gloomy and depressing day, but there was a smile on Miles' face that seemed to light up the whole big room.

Suddenly he snapped his fingers, whirled, and punched a button on his desk.

"Yes, Mr. Sullivan?" said his secretary over the intercom.

"See if you can get Bob Gunderson and Paul Hilts here for a short meeting at three o'clock." Miles knew they'd be there. They were the chief executives of IBS and as such outranked him, but Miles Sullivan was so important to the network's continuing success that he knew they'd come any time he asked. "Oh, and Miss

Barton. Arrange to have that tape from our station in Riverton, Indiana, shown on the monitor during our meeting."

Miles knew what was on the tape. He'd already seen it twice, which was the reason for the big smile on his face.

Promptly at 3:00 the two executives were escorted into the office. Miles showed them to leather-upholstered chairs in front of a TV monitor.

"Will this take long, Miles?" asked Gunderson. "I have another meeting scheduled for four."

"No. Just a few minutes, Bob. And I think you'll agree those minutes are well spent. You're about to see the birth of a television star. In fact, three television stars. If I told you what you are about to see, you'd call it ridiculous and a waste of time. So I won't say a word about it."

Miles walked over and flipped on the monitor. He punched one of five buttons beside the screen. The screen sprang to life.

Alvin Fernald, Anchorman, was seated behind his desk. A snap-brim felt hat (just like Mr. Moser wore at the Riverton *Daily Bugle*) was pushed to the back of his head. His best smile was pasted across his face.

The camera panned to Shoie, wearing a dirty baseball cap. He had a scared look on his face, and held a football as if it were a time bomb.

Shoie's face faded out and was replaced by a close-up of an enormously enlarged big toe, twitching back and forth over a crude map of the United States. The map was drawn in red crayon on the back of an old piece of wallpaper. Across the map were blue clouds, white lightning flashes, and a smiling golden sun. The toe gave one last twitch and remained motionless.

"What in blue blazes—" Bob Gunderson didn't bother to finish the sentence. He leaned forward, sitting on the very edge of the chair, a thoughtful smile on his face.

Miles punched another button, and the enormous toe stayed frozen on the screen. "What you are seeing, gentlemen, is the staff of the Junior Newsroom of our affiliate in Riverton, Indiana. They produce this news program twice each week. Their ratings in their own area are consistently higher than the ratings of 'I Love Lucy,' the 'Mary Tyler Moore Show,' or 'MASH' at their peaks. They outpull every speech of the President of the United States two to one." He paused, then said grudgingly, "Every night that they're on the air they outpull my own ratings. In the area served by the Riverton station they consistently top the ratings of the last five Superbowls, and Muhammad Ali in his greatest fight. And their ratings are still going up.

"Gentlemen, watch closely because these are our stars of tomorrow."

Miles punched another button, and the toe twitched again. The world's most famous Anchorman swung his eyes away from the screen to the eyes of the other two men.

And he had a confident smile on his face.

Phone Call from a Celebrity

11 "Alvin, somebody from New York is trying to reach you."

"Who is it?"

"Well, there's a number by the phone. You're supposed to dial that number and give them your name."

"Okay, Mom. Do I smell chocolate-chip cookies?"

"Yes. But don't eat more than two or three. I'm taking them to the PTA potluck tomorrow night. I poured a glass of milk for you. It's in the refrigerator."

"Thanks, Mom."

"Hello. Somebody said I should dial this number and give my name. My name is Alvin Byron Fernald, but I don't use the Byron much. It came from my uncle."

"Just a minute, Mr. Fernald. Mr. Sullivan has been trying to reach you for the past two hours. I think it's important."

"I was in school. I just got home. We had a history test today that was a doozy."

"A what?"

"A doozy. You know. Pretty hard."

"Oh. Well, I'll connect you with Mr. Sullivan."

"Who's Mr. Sullivan? I don't know any Mr. Sullivan. Are you sure we've both got the right numbers?"

"You know. Mr. *Miles* Sullivan."

"Oh, *that* Mr. Sullivan. The anchorman. I mean the anchorperson. The Pest makes me say that. She's my sister."

"Oh. The Pest."

"Well, I don't know Mr. Miles Sullivan, but I know who he is. Everybody knows who he is."

"Mr. Fernald, I'm connecting you with Mr. Sullivan. Go ahead, Mr. Sullivan."

"Hello, Alvin? Alvin Fernald?"

"That's me."

"I've heard great things about your work, Alvin. Your work as anchorman on the Junior News."

"Thanks Mr. Sullivan."

"Just call me Miles."

"Thanks, Miles."

"Alvin, you're doing a fabulous job out there. I've been watching the tapes of your show. They're remarkably well done. Lots of pizzazz."

"Pizzazz? I don't know what that means, Miles."

"I mean you're choosing good news stories and then really punching them up."

"Gllumphgarglemarsh."

"What? Are you still there, Alvin?"

"Glump. Garrgh. Oops. Sorry about that, Miles."

"Are you all right, Alvin?"

"Sure. I was just eating a chocolate-chip cookie while swallowing some milk."

"My favorite kind of cookie. And I'll bet yours are homemade."

"They sure are. Mom's going to take them to the PTA potluck tomorrow night."

A long silence. Then, "Chocolate-chip cookies and PTA potlucks. Alvin, you're making me homesick. Tomorrow night I have to put in an appearance at a fancy banquet thrown by one of our advertisers. I have to wear a tuxedo. I'd much rather relax in an old sweater and have some of your mother's chocolate-chip cookies."

"Hey! Why don't you come out? We'll have one of Grandpa Clifford's French-Fried Hamburgers, and then come home for the cookies."

"I'll do that some day. I promise."

A silence. Then, "Miles, isn't this costing an awful lot of money? I mean calling long distance from New York to Riverton? If you ever try to get hold of me again, why don't you call after five o'clock? Or wait until Saturday or Sunday? That reminds me. Why *did* you call?"

"Just wanted to get acquainted over the phone and tell you that I admire your work. You're doing a fine job. Please tell Shoie that I'm a sports fan, and I like his rather unusual style of sportscasting. Maybe I shouldn't tell you, Alvin, but I think the real star of your show is Daphne's toe."

"Mom makes her wash it real good just before we go to the studio."

A chuckle. "Well, Alvin, I've got to get ready for the evening news. If I can ever help you—or any of the other kids—just let me know. I've arranged to monitor all the tapes of your shows. I have a little idea running around in the back of my mind. Maybe we can talk about it the next time I call."

"Okay, Miles. But don't forget. After five or on Saturday or Sunday."

Another chuckle. "I'll try to remember, Alvin. You have my phone number, don't you?"

"Yep. Right here by the phone."

"Call that number anytime, day or night, if I can ever help you out. Whoever answers the phone will be able to locate me. Just tell them Alvin Fernald wants to talk to his friend Miles."

"Thanks, Miles. I'm real glad you called. You sound like a nice guy."

"Hope so. I have a son about your age. Maybe you two can get together before long."

"That would be neat."

"Goodbye, Alvin."

"Gurrgleshamiswah."

"What was that?"

"Another cookie."

The Junior News
Goes Network!

12 Two weeks later, Alvin Fernald, Anchor-person, watched himself become famous.

It was an eerie feeling. He was sitting in his own living room. With him, gathered for the occasion, was the entire staff of the Junior News, including Mr. Kubec. They had been told by an anonymous voice from New York that "if no big news stories break this afternoon" Miles Sullivan would use a taped segment of the kids' newscast on his nationwide program.

That program was now more than half finished, and there was no sign that the kids' tape was about to be played. Miles Sullivan, in an authoritative voice known to millions of persons ranging from presidents down to convicts, was just winding up a story about floods on the West Coast.

Alvin forced himself to pay attention. ". . . raining for five consecutive days now, adding to the problem. Half a dozen dams have already given way, and residents have been evacuated from a mountain valley 50 miles

south of San Francisco. To add to the area's woes, mudslides are beginning to bury scores of houses perched on
the mountain slopes." Alvin had visions of a river of
mud engulfing him up to his throat.

"... damage already estimated at 50 million dollars
from the mudslides alone." There was a pause, and
Miles swung his face around to peer into another camera. A smile spread across his face. It was so unusual for
Miles Sullivan to smile that everyone in the room knew
something unusual was about to happen.

"And now, a report of a different kind from the staff
of our station affiliate in Riverton, Indiana."

Miles Sullivan's face disappeared; for a split second
the tube was blank. Alvin fidgeted, then grew rigid
when his own face suddenly appeared. His "news hat"
was pushed to the back of his head. Somehow he had
already managed to wrinkle the shirt Mom had ironed
especially for the occasion. A stub of a pencil was
wedged over his right ear.

Alvin-on-TV was wearing his serious face, so Alvin-
in-the-living room put on his serious face, too. It was an
eerie feeling, watching yourself across the room talking
to you.

"Good evening, ladies and gentlemen, this is Alvin
Fernald, Anchorman of the Junior News Staff here in
Riverton.

"Flash! I have learned of a woman right here in town
who has this year alone helped more than 350 kids who
have run away from their parents or were in trouble

with the law. She's so well known among runaways that kids from all over the country come here to find her and talk over their problems. That's the way your Junior News Staff discovered her; we were told about her by a kid from Asheville, North Carolina.

"We talked to her, but she wants no publicity. We'll just call her Martha Z. She deserves a lot of help and support, and so do the kids she is helping. If you hear of kids in some kind of desperate trouble, tell them to ask the kids' information grapevine in their own town about Mrs. Z. Maybe they'll want to try to find her, here in Riverton.

"Your Junior News Team sends its salute of the week to the unknown Martha Z.

"And now, here's junior sports. Over to you, Shoie Shoemaker."

"Thanks, Alvin. The Sixth Annual Stinkbug Race was held at the high-school stadium last Saturday morning. Watch this film clip while I tell you about it. There, you're watching everybody gather around the 50-yard line. Evil Eye Davis, Willy Davis' little brother—nobody ever knew his first name, so everybody calls him Evil Eye because one stare can bring big men crashing to their knees—was umpire of the Stinkbug Race. See, now he's scratching a big circle in the dirt at the 50-yard line.

"In case you adults don't know it, stinkbugs live in the rotten bark of dead trees, and if you squish them they stink something awful.

"Now watch! There's the beginning of the race! See? Everybody drops their stinkbugs in the middle of the circle. They've painted them different colors so they don't get mixed up.

"Now watch the close-up. There goes Skinny Mulroy's stinkbug out in front. Looks like it's a winner. Ooooops! That was awful. Dick Teresi wasn't watching where he was going, and stepped on Skinny's stinkbug. Everybody's backing up, holding their noses.

"Now watch. Here comes Skinny Mulroy with a mad look on his face. Skinny pokes his elbow into Dick Teresi's ribs. Teresi's left shoots out and begins to pull hair. There goes Evil Eye's stare!"

"Well, that's all of the film we're going to show on the air. We've given the rest of it a CG rating, and you parents can see it with your child's permission."

"Folks, next week I'm going to show you the final test flight of the five-man hang glider that the Morris twins and some of the other kids are building over on Walnut Street. It's really neat. They're using hickory branches for the framework and covering it with some big sheets of plastic left over after they built the new chicken restaurant out on Highway 30. They'll launch from Scheunemann's Hill sometime next weekend. Hang in there, kids! Over to you, Alvin."

"Thanks, Shoie. Now, a new feature of the Junior News. We present 'On the Road with Worm Wormley.' Worm used to stutter, but he's been doing real good this year. Haven't you, Worm?"

"I g-g-g-guess so, Alvin. In my search for the unusual

this week I d-d-dug up this kid named Carrots Johann-sen. Carrots is a memory freak. What I mean is, Carrots just don't forget nothin'.

"Now here I am on film, standing beside Carrots. He hasn't got a very big head, and it isn't p-p-p-pointy or anything, considering everything he remembers in it. Carrots doesn't have any idea what questions I'm going to ask. Do you, Carrots?"

"Naw."

"Now, I'm going to give you a batch of numbers. 378–542–984–432–7."

"Got it."

"Okay, now how old are you, Carrots?"

"Ten."

"Who hit a two-bagger to send in the winning run in the Grade School Softball Championship five years ago?"

"Judy Phipps. One of three girls who ever made the team. Mole on the left side of her neck. Jiggled when she ran."

"How many sycamore trees are there between First and Fifth avenues?"

"Nineteen. One dead. Five had bird's nests this year. Four robins. One wren."

"Each year the Methodist Ladies' Auxiliary has a glass jar filled with beans at the county fair. How many beans were in that jar three years ago?"

"Two thousand eight hundred twenty-one. Bill Simmons won the prize. Five dollars. Wearing white buck-skin shoes."

"You certainly have a remarkable memory. Can you explain it?"

"Carrots."

"Carrots?"

"Carrots. I like 'em. Eat lots of carrots, every day. Anybody eats carrots, they remember things."

"What was that number I gave you when this interview started?"

"378–542–984–432–7. You paused and took a breath just before the seven."

"I pause so I d-d-don't stutter. Carrots, what's your phone number?"

". . . . . Doggone . . . . Can't remember. Not very important."

"Over to you, Alvin."

"Okay, folks. Let's see what the weather has in store for us. Here's Weatherperson Daphne Fernald."

"You folks out there watching the network show may not know that I have a special big toe that tells me what the weather will be, like my toe gets hot or cold, or sore or stiff, and sometimes it crinks when I bend it. Each one of those things means something to me as a Weatherperson. See? Here's my toe up on the stool. I took off my sock so you could see it. Good ol' toe. It's hot, and stiff, and about 45 minutes ago it crinked. That means tomorrow will be cool and dry, but there'll be clouds most of the day, and it'll be pretty warm for this time of year, but take along a warm sweater, especially if you go to the courthouse, where they're keeping the temperature mighty low these days, and everybody's grumbling about it except Mr. Price, who is a very hot-blooded

man. Just walking around out in the snow, Mr. Price
sweats up a short-sleeved shirt something awful. Sometime I'll tell you more about Mr. Price.

"Now here's two of my famous 'Daphne Observes'
sayings: Daphne observes that you can't trust a man
with skinny ankles. Also, Daphne observes that popcorn
can solve almost any problem. Over to you, Alvin."

"You didn't tell me you were going to do that
'Daphne Observes' bit. You should be ashamed.

"And now, folks, for this Anchorperson's commentary. According to Miss Kapp over at our library, there
are more than 75 million kids under 18 in this country. I
figure each of them buys an average of three pairs of
shoes every year. That's a total of 225 million new pairs
of shoes per year. Now, half the shoes those new ones
replace aren't worn out. They're just outgrown. That
means there are approximately 122,500,000 pairs of
perfectly good shoes available to the other kids of this
country every year, if we can find some way to dis-
tribute them.

"This Anchorperson proposes that the federal gov-
ernment start a Department of Used Children's Shoes.
Every town of any size would have a place where kids
could turn in shoes they'd outgrown, and choose from a
zillion other new shoes that fit. The kids would like this
setup, and, estimating the average value of a used pair
of shoes at ten dollars—which is certainly low—the Department of Used Children's Shoes would save parents
of this country about one and a half billion dollars each
year. *One and a half billion dollars!*

"If this nation can afford a Department of Defense,

and a Department of Commerce, and a Department of Interior—whatever they are—then it certainly can afford a Department of Used Children's Shoes.

"And that's the way your Junior News Staff sees it, this 18th day of November. Back to you, Miles Sullivan."

Fame Turns Sour

13 Alvin Fernald had often dreamed of being famous, but never did he dream of the fame he achieved as a result of the network telecast. And it turned his life around—for the worse.

The phone rang constantly for two days. At least half a dozen theatrical agents called, trying to handle his career on TV or promising to make him a movie star. A country-and-western music group wanted him to narrate a record about an escaped convict while they played banjos or zithers in the background. Dozens of publicity agents called, trying to plant plugs for their specific products in the Junior News air time.

Mom and Dad worried about all the attention Alvin was getting.

"Don't stew about it," he said airily. "They're just looking for a piece of the action. I know how to handle those jokers." His self-confident words didn't seem to reassure his parents in the least. In fact, they seemed still more worried.

He had a dozen calls, at various times of the night, from girls who had seen him on television and developed a sudden crush. He pretended to hate these particular calls; secretly, he enjoyed them. On one occasion he took the phone into the hall closet and closed the door so he could talk privately with a husky-voiced girl from Wheaton, Illinois, named M. Sue.

Daphne and Shoie received their share of attention, too. A messenger delivered to Daphne a package containing three dozen pairs of socks, with a note from the manufacturer that she had the "sexiest little toe on television." The head of the U.S. Weather Bureau personally called to congratulate her on the accuracy of her forecasts.

The Dallas Cowgirls voted Shoie the "sportscaster we'd most like to date," and the daughter of a shipping millionaire called from Greece and asked Shoie if he'd fly over and play volleyball with her.

The kids wore their fame pretty well—except for Alvin. He became cockier and cockier, and at one point cleared the shelf above the fireplace "to make room for the Emmy I'm sure to win this year."

Alvin, to tell the truth, had become a pain in the neck. Everyone complained in private about his airy conceit, about how difficult it was to get along with him anymore.

It was Mr. Kubec who did something about it. He found an opportunity after an afternoon story conference at the studio. He asked Alvin to stay behind and discuss some new camera angles. Mr. Kubec led the way into his tiny office. He closed the door, put his feet up on a battered desk, leaned back in his chair, and suddenly looked straight at Alvin. He stared without blinking for a full minute. Then he said, "By now we're old friends, Alvin. We can speak frankly to each other, can't we?"

"Sure. About the camera angles? I think my left profile is more interesting than my right profile."

"No. Not about camera angles. About *you*, Alvin. I'm worried about *you*."

Alvin opened his mouth to speak, but Mr. Kubec held up a hand.

"You're a good kid. One of the finest boys I've ever known. But you're letting all this TV stuff go to your head. You're beginning to *act* the part of a bigshot. And when any child begins to *act* a part, it means he's in trouble. He's not being himself."

Suddenly Mr. Kubec whipped his feet to the floor, slammed forward on his chair, and leaned toward Alvin.

"This TV business could ruin your life. Your entire life. It just isn't worth that. Let me tell you something. When I was living in Santa Maria, I knew a boy whose mother pushed him into the movies. She was successful, too. Successful at ruining his life. He began *acting* the part of a movie star. And he began running around with older kids who were acting out their *own* parts, of one kind or another. I read about him in the paper last week. He was sentenced to prison on a drug charge. A nice lad—who suddenly became famous."

Alvin swallowed. There was silence in the little office. Then, "I guess maybe you're right. I didn't know I was getting so stuck-up. Have the other kids noticed it?"

"Pete has. We've talked about it."

"Well, I . . . Well, I'll try to come back down to earth.

Maybe you'll help. Anyway I'm glad you told me, Mr. Kubec."

"So am I, Alvin. So am I."

A breath of fresh air blew through the Magnificent Brain. Alvin suddenly found his thoughts shifting from himself to the other kids, to Mr. Kubec. It was a relief to be Alvin Fernald again, instead of a famous anchorman. Anchorperson. At that moment he liked Mr. Kubec enormously.

And suddenly Alvin became very curious about the man.

"Tell me about *yourself*, Mr. Kubec. Where did you live and what did you do before you came to Riverton?"

Mr. Kubec stood up. "There's nothing to tell, Alvin. Nothing that would interest you, or anyone else." He seemed flustered. "You'd better run for home. Your parents will be looking for you."

The conversation straightened Alvin out in a hurry, but it also deepened his interest in Mr. Kubec. Who was the man? Where was he from? What had he done in his past?

Casually, as though it were unimportant, Alvin began asking questions around town. He learned that Mr. Kubec had first appeared in Riverton about four years ago, that he lived by himself in a small apartment above Mike Shuck's billiard parlor, and that he ate most of his meals sitting at the counter in McAllister's Drugstore. And that was all he found out. Everyone *liked* Mr. Kubec, but no one knew anything about him.

The puzzle of Mr. Kubec's background became an

obsession to Alvin. He tried trapping the man into making statements about himself—with absolutely no success. He wondered about Mr. Kubec in school, in bed at night, even when he was in the middle of a telecast. Every time the red camera light blinked on, Alvin asked himself questions about the man behind it.

Then one morning, as he was dressing for school, the Magnificent Brain came up with a random thought that was to unravel the mystery. What had Mr. Kubec said in his office that day he had talked to Alvin? "When I lived in Santa Maria I knew a boy . . ." *Santa Maria?*

That same afternoon Alvin stopped in and asked Mrs. Kapp, his favorite librarian, where a town named Santa Maria was located.

It took her about three minutes to find the answer. "Alvin, there are at least half a dozen Santa Marias scattered around the Western Hemisphere. There's one in Chile, Brazil, Colombia, and a Santa Maria volcano in Guatemala. But the Santa Maria you may be looking for is Santa Maria, California—a small city located about seventy-five miles south of San Francisco. I can tell you where to find out more about it if you want me to, Alvin. Is this for a school report?"

"No. No, not exactly. It's for another kind of report, though."

A knowing look came into Mrs. Kapp's eyes. "Oh. I see. Something to do with your television program. Right?"

"That's right, Mrs. Kapp. And thanks for your help." He smiled. "I thank you. Miles Sullivan thanks you. And thirty million viewers thank you." Alvin couldn't help hinting at his own importance, despite his conversation with Mr. Kubec.

Mrs. Kapp smiled back.

Alvin took his Dad's Polaroid camera to the TV studio that afternoon. He made a great show of taking candid pictures of Shoie, the Pest, Pete, even Mr. Bessimer, who hrrmphed several times, then practiced saying "cheese" for 30 seconds before he'd let Alvin snap the shutter.

But when Alvin tried to get Mr. Kubec to pose, the man muttered, "Not now, Alvin. Too busy," and walked away.

A little later, though, while Mr. Kubec was busy adjusting the TV camera, Alvin snapped a photo of him without his knowledge. It was a profile shot, a little too far away for Alvin's purpose, but not bad considering his problems in getting it.

The last thing Alvin did before going to bed that night was to write a letter. He enclosed the snapshot of Mr. Kubec. The letter read:

Anchorman
IBS News
Santa Maria, California

Dear Sir or Anchorperson:

The man in the accompanying photo now lives in Riverton, Indiana. His name is John

Kubec. I have information that he may have lived in Santa Maria several years ago. Any information you can provide will be helpful.

> *Yours truly,*
> *Alvin Fernald*
> ~~Anchorman~~ Anchorperson
> IBS News
> Riverton, Indiana

A Million Dollars
Vanishes—Poof!

 "Alvin, there's a phone call for you. It's long distance."

"Coming, Mom."

"I swear I'm going to take that phone off the wall if people don't stop calling you from all over the world."

As he took the phone from her he tickled her in a secret tickle-spot under her left ear, a tickle-spot he'd discovered so long ago he couldn't remember.

"Alvin, stop that!" she said with a giggle, slapping his hand.

"Hello. Alvin Fernald here. Who's there?"

"Alvin Fernald, this is Scott Lewis. I'm manager of the IBS newsroom in Santa Maria, California. I called your station in Riverton, and they gave me your home phone number. I hope you don't mind me calling you at home."

"Of course not." Alvin's brain snapped to attention the instant he heard the name Santa Maria.

"It's great for an old geezer in the TV biz, like me, to

talk to a young'un who's already famous, like you, Alvin. I caught your segment—the one on the Miles Sullivan show. It was a smash. A real smasheroo."

"Thanks, Scott. Did you get my letter?"

"I especially liked the girl who plays the part of the weatherman. Such talent! Where did you dig her up?"

"First noticed her about eight years ago. Did you get my letter, Scott?"

"And that sports guy is a knockout. You've got a top-notch professional team there, Alvin."

"Doggone it, Scott, did you get my letter?"

"Yep. That's the sign of a real professional. You get right down to business. Always thinking about the big story. Right, Alvin?"

"Yep, yourself. I'm glad you called, Scott, but *why* did you call?"

"It's about this guy John Kubec, Alvin. You've got a blockbuster of a story there. A real smasheroo. Where'd your tip come from?"

"What do you mean, tip?"

"You know. Who tipped you off that the guy is in Riverton? Did you inform the FBI yet?"

Alvin thought furiously. Finally he said, "No, not yet, Scott. I, well, I want to get a little deeper into the story before I do that. What do you know about John Kubec?"

"I know that his name isn't John Kubec. The man in that photograph lived here in Santa Maria for six years. His real name is John Kolsky. He's a convicted bank robber who served time in the penitentiary."

Alvin was stunned. "Bank robber?"

"Yes. I thought you knew. After serving six years of his stretch he was paroled. As soon as he was off parole, he vanished. No trace. But the FBI is still interested in his whereabouts."

"Why?"

"Well, the bank loot was never recovered. Almost a million dollars. When last seen it was in a stolen armored truck. That truck disappeared, Alvin. Puff! Into thin air. Can you imagine an armored truck disappearing without a trace? Beyond belief. Anyway, that's why the FBI still is interested in John Kolsky, alias John Kubec. Even though he's served his time, and they can't charge him with anything more, they figure that sooner or later he'll make his move toward the bank loot. Then they'll recover it. Can you imagine knowing where a million bucks is stashed away, and not daring to go near it?"

"No, I can't. I can't imagine any of this."

"Well, if Mr. John Kolsky is about to make his move toward that loot, you've got a smasheroo of a story, Alvin. A smasheroo. How about sharing it with me?"

"Well. Well, I'll let you know if I find out anything. Thanks for calling, Scott."

"Let's share the story, old buddy. You develop your end, and I'll stir into things out here. We'll come up with a blockbuster. Maybe it'll even make the Miles Sullivan national news. I've never managed to get anything on the Miles Sullivan show yet. Maybe we can work this into something hot."

"Maybe."

"Most fascinating thing about the story is the armored truck carrying a million dollars. Vanished into thin air. Poof. You find out what happened to that truck, Alvin, and you'll nail down a smasheroo."

"Thanks for your help, Scott. Goodbye."

"You're welcome, old buddy. Anytime. Keep this old geezer posted. Hey, I just thought of something! How about sending me an autographed picture of yourself, Alvin? My kids would love it."

"I'll see what I can do. Goodbye, Scott."

"Goodbye, old buddy."

Alvin didn't sleep much that night.

Face to Face
with a Convict

15 A convicted bank robber! A man who had stolen a million dollars, and now knew where it was hidden!

Alvin tried to believe it, but couldn't. There must be some mistake. Mr. Kubec was too nice a guy to be a criminal.

Late the next afternoon the Junior News Staff was taping an interview with Beetle Larson, who had taught himself to play the guitar and now had organized a rock group called the Unwashed Flying Squirrels. During the taping Alvin tried to act as natural as possible around Mr. Kubec. No luck. He found that he couldn't look the man in the eye; and whenever he said anything to Mr. Kubec, his voice was a high-pitched squeak.

Finally he decided he had to do *something*. He couldn't stand this mental upset much longer. He had to learn the truth.

After the taping session was over, when the other kids were heading for the door, Alvin headed toward Mr. Kubec. "You going to walk home now?"

"Yes. Unless you have something else you want to shoot."

"Mind if I walk along with you?"

"Of course not. I'd enjoy it, Alvin."

Outside, it was a gray, depressing day. Dark clouds scudded low across the sky. There was a strong taste of winter in the air. *Fine. The day just matches my mood*, thought Alvin.

They walked up Main Street, then turned left through Weasel Park along the river. Mr. Kubec glanced sideways at Alvin. "Anything particular on your mind?"

"No, not at all. Nothing at all." The words popped out too fast.

They walked in silence. Then Mr. Kubec said, "There's something bothering you, Alvin. You're not hiding it very well."

Alvin stopped dead in his tracks. "Are you a bank robber, Mr. Kubec?" he blurted.

The man staggered as though he'd been struck. He reached out to a tree for support. His normally cheery face looked much older.

"How did you find out about me?" he asked in a whisper.

"Then it's true? You *are* a bank robber?"

"No, Alvin. It's *not* true. And you must tell absolutely no one in Riverton anything you've learned about me."

Alvin looked at him suspiciously.

"Let's sit on the bench over there, Alvin. We have some talking to do."

The wind seemed even sharper when they sat down. Alvin waited for the man to pick up the conversation.

"What do you know about me, Alvin? And where did you get your information?"

"That's exactly the trouble. I didn't know *anything* about you. And I thought you were such a nice guy that I got sort of curious, and decided to find out more about you. There's nothing wrong in that."

Mr. Kubec sighed. "No. There's nothing wrong in that."

A maple leaf floated down and crossed in front of Alvin's nose.

"Well, I wrote a letter to the IBS newsroom in Santa Maria. A guy named Scott Lewis called me, and told me all about you. About how you robbed a bank, and served six years in the penitentiary. And how the armored truck vanished with a million dollars in it. And how you still know where the loot is hidden. And the FBI wants to know where you are."

"Have you told Pete what you found out? Or any of the other kids?"

"No." As soon as he replied, Alvin felt a chill of danger. He was the only person who knew the man's secret.

"I'm going to tell you the story of my life, Alvin. And when I'm through, I'm going to leave it up to you whether you tell anyone else that story, or whether it remains a long-buried secret."

A Secret Life

 "Peter is my son." He made the statement flatly, with no emotion in his voice.

Alvin was so stunned he could think of nothing to say.

"My real son," repeated Mr. Kubec. "When Peter was born, his mother and I lived in Santa Maria, California.

"Those were the happiest days of my life. I was an X-ray technician at the hospital there. That was where I met Peter's mother, Alicia. She worked as a nurse in the hospital. She was a beautiful girl, a radiant girl. I suppose she grows more beautiful each day in my mind. I suppose that she was not really as beautiful as I now see her. But I find that difficult to believe. She was so *alive*, Alvin. It was almost as though she had her own sun, shining inside her.

"We had been married three years, three years so happy I can't describe them, when Peter was conceived. There were complications from the start, and by the time Peter was born, Alicia was worn and wasted. Even though she was pregnant, most of her body had grown thin and weak.

"Alicia died three hours after Peter was born."

The wind rustled the maple tree. Alvin stared down at the toe of his right shoe. There was a tightness in his throat.

"Although Alicia died, Peter lived. He was a fine healthy baby, as though somehow he had absorbed the radiance that had been his mother's. I hired a widow to take care of him while I worked.

"I no longer could face going each day to the hospital where Alicia had died. Within a few weeks I quit my job, and started looking for another. This was during a recession, and jobs were not very plentiful. My money ran out, and I borrowed from a loan company to pay our debts, and to pay the lady who was taking care of Peter.

"Finally I landed a job as a guard at a bank in Santa Maria. That was a black day for me, for the job led me straight into prison.

"The worst day of my life was April the eighteenth, eleven years ago. It was a dark, rainy day, much like this one. In fact, it had been raining steadily for five days. On the morning of April the eighteenth, two gunmen, unbeknownst to me, seized an armored truck. They tied up the driver and his assistant, and dumped them out on a country road. Oh, they were very clever, those two. Instead of seizing an armored truck *full* of money, when the guards would be alert, they seized an *empty* one, when the guards were not particularly watchful. Then they used the truck and the guards' uniforms as a means of obtaining the money.

"They entered the bank where I worked with empty

bags over their arms; the guards did this every morning. One walked directly up to me and lifted the bag off his hand. I saw a gun pointed at my stomach. 'Hand over your revolver or I'll start shooting—you and everyone else,' he said in a low voice. I did as the manager had instructed me to do when I took the job. 'Always put a life, including your own, ahead of any amount of money in the bank,' he'd said.

"I gave him my revolver. Then, shouting loudly to scare people, the two men lined up everyone in the bank against one wall. They threatened to shoot people, one by one, if their orders weren't instantly obeyed. One of the men stayed there, with his gun sweeping back and forth. The other man tossed me an empty bag. He ordered me to walk into the vault ahead of him and to fill the bag with money, from five-dollar bills to hundred-dollar bills. When I didn't move, he fired a shot into the floor. I ran for the vault.

"In all, they took out six bags of money. They made me carry four of the bags to the armored truck outside, while each of them carried one bag so he could keep a gun-hand free.

"As we were leaving the bank one of the men shouted at the people inside, 'There's another of us in a second-floor window across the street. He has a high-powered rifle. He can see every inch of this room through the front windows. Anyone who makes a move in the next fifteen minutes—anyone who even scratches his nose—is instantly dead.'

"I thought my ordeal was over when I shoved the

money bags inside the back of the truck. I wasn't so lucky. They shoved me around the truck and inside the cab. I sat in the seat beside the driver. One of the men jumped behind the wheel and the other into the back of the truck."

A small bug crawled across the toe of Alvin's shoe. Alvin was afraid to say a word.

"An armored truck is built with a gun-slit facing from the rear into the driver's cab, so the guard in the rear can aid the driver up front in case of any trouble. I sat there in the front seat with a gun at the back of my head while those two thieves made their escape. They obviously were holding me hostage in case they ran into any trouble.

"But why should there be any trouble? The terrified people in the bank would eventually sound the alarm, but not for several minutes if they thought they'd be shot if they made a move. And who would suspect that armed bandits were making their escape in an armored car? Oh, those two were clever.

"The man beside me drove as though he'd rehearsed the drive a thousand times. Within three minutes we were on the outskirts of town, and five minutes later we were heading up a lonely canyon road. I didn't see a single car on that weed-filled road.

"No matter where they were going, they'd sooner or later have to dispose of me, I figured. That idea didn't have much appeal. I began thinking desperately of a way to escape.

"We were rounding a mountain curve when the two men got into an argument over what to do with the guards' uniforms. I figured it was my only chance because their attention had shifted away from me. I took a slow, deep breath and began counting.

"On the count of three, at the sharpest part of the curve, I ducked my head, jerked open the door, and rolled out. For some reason I continued counting, now shouting out the numbers. I somersaulted down the mountain and crashed into an orange-colored boulder on the count of fourteen. I looked up, dazed, just in time to see the armored truck pick up speed as it disappeared around the curve. I guess they figured they didn't need a hostage any longer."

By now the bug had crawled up Alvin's shoe, across his sock, and was climbing up his leg. He reached down and flicked it away.

"Nobody ever saw the gunmen or the truck again.

"The rest of my story is quite short, Alvin. I found my way back to Santa Maria and walked into the police station. I told them exactly what had happened. From the first they regarded me with suspicion, and called in the FBI. They had a good case, I guess. I'd been working at the bank only a few days. The robbery depended on inside information, they said, and I had such information. When they found out I was heavily in debt, because of Alicia and Peter, their case was even stronger.

"I was convicted in a trial that lasted less than one day. Twenty years, said the judge.

"It was strange, Alvin. When I went to prison I wasn't bitter. Instead, all my thoughts were on Peter, and how he could be taken care of.

"There were no immediate relatives on Alicia's side of the family, nor on mine. Alicia had mentioned, a couple of times, an aunt and uncle who lived in Indiana. I asked for help from the social worker who visited the prison. She was able to locate Mildred and Fred Waters—Pete's great-aunt and great-uncle here in Riverton. By phone she told them the truth about Alicia, but said that I had disappeared after Alicia's death. As you know, Alvin, they are good people. Immediately they agreed to take Peter in, and they have raised him in a fine, loving home.

"After six years of good behavior I was paroled. I had to stay in the state another six months so I could report to the parole officer. The day I went off parole I headed for Riverton.

"I didn't want Pete to know that his father had served time in prison—even though I was innocent—so I buried my past as completely as I could. It seemed best not to let Pete know who I was. He was happy with the Waters; why should I interfere? So I found a job at the TV station, and watched Pete grow up.

"I made a good friend of Peter. I made a good friend of my own son. He's a fine boy, Alvin. I'm so proud of my son."

Another leaf sailed past Alvin's eyes, but he could hardly see it. There seemed to be a mist everywhere.

Alvin cleared his throat. "Don't worry, Mr. Kubec. I'll keep your secret."

Mr. Kubec squeezed his shoulder.

A minute passed in total silence. Then Alvin couldn't resist a final question. "Do you have any idea what happened to the money?"

"No. The last time I saw the armored truck it was rounding a curve going up the canyon road. Almost at the top of the canyon, hidden in an aspen grove, the police found a car belonging to one of the gunmen. It must have been their getaway car, but it obviously hadn't been used. The armored truck apparently never reached the grove. The police searched that part of the mountains thoroughly, but never found a trace of it. I've often been tempted to go back and search the canyon myself. But I don't dare."

"Why not?"

"Suppose I were successful, Alvin. Suppose through sheer luck I found the truck, with the loot still inside. It would only be evidence that I was *guilty*, not *innocent*. No, I don't dare go anywhere near that canyon."

Another long silence.

"Thanks for sharing my secret, Alvin. I feel better just talking it out with you. And thanks for *keeping* it a secret, too."

Alvin cleared his throat. "Someday you'll be cleared of that crime. Someday Pete will know you're his father. He *should* know. And maybe that someday isn't far away. There's no telling what an anchorperson can do."

The Magnificent Brain
Comes Through!

17 From the moment Alvin heard Mr. Kubec's story, everything went from bad to worse. Alvin walked around in a daze. His mind was constantly on Pete and Mr. Kubec. The Magnificent Brain was a flop. It failed to function in school. On the air it seemed to short-circuit anything Alvin was supposed to say.

And whenever something went wrong on the Junior News Staff, tempers flared. The other kids became almost as edgy as Alvin.

At one point the Pest stormed out of the studio because "my toe isn't getting enough air time." The other kids could depend on Shoie to be 15 minutes late to any taping session, which upset Pete, whose job as director was to coordinate the whole staff.

And when Pete was upset, Mr. Kubec became visibly shaken.

From bad to still worse.

Alvin tried half-heartedly to patch up the world that

was falling apart around him, but he felt like he was on a merry-go-round going faster and faster, and that inevitably he would fly off.

At one point he simply couldn't find the time—or the desire—to rake the leaves, a job Dad had assigned to him in no uncertain terms. This caused words at the dinner table, which in turn upset Mom. "Sometimes I wish you had never become an anchorman, Alvin."

"Anchorperson, Mom," said the Pest."

"Nobody understands anything," said Alvin, getting to his feet and heading for his room. "Can't a guy be so busy he forgets something simple like a few leaves? Criminy!"

"Come back and finish your dinner," ordered his father.

"I'm not hungry."

Up in his room, he closed the door and cocked the Foolproof Burglar Alarm. He placed his back against the wall and slid down until he was sitting on the floor, knees up in front of his face. The Magnificent Brain had some work to do.

"Criminy!" he said again, aloud.

He closed his eyes, not to sleep, but so he could concentrate. His hand went up and tugged gently on the lobe of his right ear.

The Magnificent Brain switched on.

A gray screen swept across in front of Alvin's closed eyes. Whenever the Brain came up with great ideas, that screen was ripped and torn by crackling yellow bolts of lightning, and Alvin heard strange hums and squeaks in his ears.

Concentrate.

World is falling apart around. Nobody understands. Television no fun anymore. Pete and Mr. Kubec. Father and son. Must straighten that out somehow. Good guys. Prove him innocent. That most important thing. Must prove him innocent. Then maybe everything else all right.

Big armored truck vanished. Amazing. How could big truck vanish? Find that out, maybe prove Mr. Kubec innocent, then everything all right again. Like to meet that girl named M. Sue who called me from Wheaton, Illinois.

Hey! How'd that girl get in here?

Keep mind on important stuff. Most important, how did armored truck vanish?

Truck moves up deserted mountain road, rounds corner. Disappears. Maybe driver goofs, truck rolls off road and down side of mountain. But police would find it.

Something strange here. Something strange about that day. April eighteenth. Eleven years ago. Strange about that day.

(A small lightning bolt shot down from the top and ripped a short distance across the gray screen. Alvin instantly reached up and tugged his earlobe again.)

Good. Brain beginning to work. Hearing a few hums and beeps. Beeps a good sign. Beeps come faster and faster, suddenly change into siren. Then lots of flashes, lots of ideas.

Good ol' Brain.

How truck vanish? What happened to gunmen? Something sticks in good ol' Brain about day of robbery. Something about the day. About the day.

Beep. Beep.

Beep-beep-beep.

Wail of siren. Flashes, blinding lights, thunder, the whole screen alight with fireworks. Roman candles and skyrockets.

A tremendous bang. The screen turns bright red.

Alvin's eyes flew wide open.

That's it! That *must* be it! He had the key that would unlock the mystery! He had the key that would give Pete and Mr. Kubec a whole new life together.

Plans for a
Real Smasheroo

 "This meeting will come to order," said Alvin.

"But Pete's not here yet," said the Pest.

"And why aren't we meeting at the TV studio, like we usually do?" asked Shoie.

"This meeting will come to order," repeated Alvin. "It isn't a regular meeting. It's a meeting of just the three of us because we have a lot of important planning to do. Pete and Mr. Kubec weren't invited to attend."

"Why not?" asked Shoie.

"Why not?" echoed the Pest.

Alvin held up his hand. He was lying on his side on his bed. Shoie was sitting on the stool in front of Alvin's Inventing Bench, and Daphne squatted on the floor in a yoga position she had been practicing. It pained Alvin to see her tied in such a knot.

"Be patient, you guys. We are faced with the biggest story we've ever handled."

Daphne's eyes peeped out from behind an ankle.

"What's the story, Alvin? Sounds interesting."

"I can't tell you the whole story because I've been sworn to secrecy. It's the biggest story I ever heard of, and it's also the biggest secret of my life."

"If it's such a big story, why aren't we talking it over with Pete and Mr. Kubec?" asked Shoie. "They're directing the show."

"They aren't here because they're a part of the story itself. A big part."

"You mean they'll be in the news?"

"Yes. In a big way, a very big way. They'll probably be on the Miles Sullivan show."

"Oh, Alvin. That sounds so exciting! Tell us more."

"I can't. As I said, I've been sworn to secrecy. You guys have trusted me in the past. This time you'll have to *really* trust me. In order to cover this story there are some things I need to know. So I need your help."

"If we cover the story, will it make Pete happy?" The Pest was now standing on her head in the corner. "He's not been much fun the last few days. Oops. Lost my bubble gum. Will you hand it to me, Shoie?"

Shoie reached over and popped her gum into her mouth.

"Yes, it will make Pete *very* happy. Happier than he's ever been in his life."

"Then I'll do whatever you ask, Alvin."

"Count on me, old bean," said Shoie. "But I sure wish you'd tell us what this is all about."

"No can do. But I promise that some day you'll know. Now let's do some planning. Pest, how well do you know the Director of the U.S. Weather Service?"

"Pretty good. He called me, and talked to me for forty-five minutes. Said he'd like to rent my weather toe, but he didn't think he could get the money from Congress. Said I reminded him of his own daughter when she was my age. We talked about the weather, and school, and why frogs are green instead of orange, and the right way to trim your toenails. All kinds of things like that."

"Do you think if you called him in Washington that you could get through to him?"

"No sweat." It was a phrase she'd heard some of the boys at school use, and she'd liked it. "He said to call him anytime."

"Good. I want you to ask him for this information." He took a piece of paper from his pocket and put it between her upturned feet. She swung gracefully down into her original yoga position, reached up behind her neck, and took the paper from between her toes. She read it.

"No sweat," she said again.

"Now, Shoie, I want you to ride your bike out to Scheunemann's Hill."

"Who do I see out there?"

"You don't *see* anybody. You *do* something."

"What do I do?"

"You take along a tape measure and a stake. Drive the stake in the ground at the top of the hill. Then you come riding along on your bike as fast as you can. Count steadily to three. Suddenly when you reach the stake you dive off the bike and roll down the hill while you keep on counting to fourteen fairly fast. Then you measure the distance from the point where you hollered 'fourteen' back up to the stake."

"You must be out of your mind, old man. You're flaky. No way I'll do that."

"Oh, come on," said the Pest. "You're the best athlete at Roosevelt. And the best sportscaster in the world. Besides, Alvin says it will help out Pete and Mr. Kubec."

The flattery reached him. "Okay, okay. I'll do it. But it doesn't make sense."

"Do it three times," said Alvin, "so we'll know that it's accurate. Give me the average distance."

"You mean I'm going to have to flang myself off the bike and roll down that steep hill three times?"

"Orders from the anchorman," said Alvin.

"I'll sue if I get hurt," Shoie grumbled.

"Okay, let's get this news team into action," said Alvin. "I have some telephoning to do myself, and I don't dare use the phone at the studio because somebody might hear. Pest, you make your call to the Weather Bureau first, while I do a little more planning. Shoie, you go out and make your Dive of Death."

Shoie shuddered. "Did you have to call it that?"

After Daphne had completed her call, Alvin took over the phone. He dialed a long-distance number. "Hello, I want to talk to Scott Lewis."

"Who's calling, please?"

"Alvin Fernald, IBS anchorman in Riverton, Indiana."

"Do you mean anchor*person*?"

"You're as bad as my sister."

"I'll get Mr. Lewis for you."

"Scott Lewis here. Hi, Alvin. Good to hear from you."

"Hi, Scott. This call is costing lots of money, and I'm calling from my home because I can't use the studio phone. I have Mom's egg timer in front of me so I won't talk too long. I just turned it over, and the sand is beginning to run through. I want you to do a favor for me, and in return I'll give you a piece of the biggest story you've ever covered."

"The Kubec-Kolsky thing?"

"Right. Now here's what I want you to do . . ."

Three minutes later the last grains of sand ran through the egg timer. "That's about it, Scott. Will you do all that for me?"

Scott Lewis gave a long, low whistle. "You sure do want a lot, Alvin. Are you sure you know what you're doing?"

"Yep. Absolutely."

"And I can have this end of the story all to myself?"

"Absolutely."

"Okay, I'll do it. But this is going to take quite a lot of money, Alvin. Who's going to pay for it?"

"Miles Sullivan."

"Wow! So he's locked into this story!"

"Nope. Not yet. He doesn't know anything about the story. But he's going to agree to pay the costs."

"I'll ask you once more, Alvin. Do you know what you're doing?"

"Absolutely."

"Well, I'll get things moving out here. I assume I'll be hearing from you—and from Miles Sullivan—sometime tomorrow."

"Absolutely."

"That story's going to be a smasheroo, Alvin. A real smasheroo."

"My secretary said you called while I was out." The voice familiar to millions boomed in Alvin's ear. "Good to hear from you, Alvin."

"Thanks for returning my call, Miles."

"You've become mighty famous, Alvin. How are things going out there?"

"Fine. Miles, these long-distance calls are costing a lot of money, so I'd like to get right to business. I've got Mom's egg timer here so I won't run over three minutes."

Laughter crackled in his ear. "Alvin, call me collect anytime you want."

"Thanks, Miles. Do you remember once you offered to help me out in any way you could?"

"Of course. What can I do for you?"

"Well, I'm developing the biggest story of my life. I want you to put it on your show tomorrow night, Friday, without seeing any tape first. I want you to put it on *live*."

A whistle. "Well, I don't know about that, Alvin. What's this big story about?"

"I can't tell you because I'm pledged to secrecy."

A long pause.

"Miles, about half the sand has run through the timer."

"Alvin, you'll have to give me more to go on than this."

A short pause. Then Alvin blurted, "It's about a bank robbery, a million dollars missing, an armored truck that vanishes into thin air, and a boy who finds a father he doesn't even know is alive."

"All that in just one story?"

"Yes. It's a real smasheroo."

Another long pause. "I must be out of my mind, Alvin. I'm risking my whole career on you, but I trust you. I think I'll do it."

"If anything goes wrong, all you have to do is flip a switch and put some other story on the tube."

"You're right. Okay, I'll do it."

"One more thing, Miles. Will you call Scott Lewis in the IBS newsroom in Santa Maria, California, and tell him to give me all the help he can? And tell him that the network will pay for it?"

"I *am* out of my mind. Yes, I'll call him as soon as we hang up."

"Good. Hang up quick. The sand just ran out."

"That's the Way Your Anchorman Sees It..."

19 "... heavy trading on the stock market today, with the Dow-Jones average declining by eight points." It was Miles Sullivan's voice.

Alvin fidgeted at his desk. The spots and floodlights glared brightly at him. He was about to cover the biggest story of his career, and he had no idea how he'd do it.

Thirty million people would be watching, and he might fall flat on his face.

He'd tried to prepare a script for the show, then thrown away the half-page of scrawled notes. Instinct told him that this story had to be covered live and unrehearsed.

He had asked Don Brooks to be in the control room to direct the show. He knew he could rely on Don's experience as an anchorman. He hoped Don could keep up with the story without rehearsal, and would cue in the tapes and remotes at the proper time.

He'd simply told everyone except Don that he had arranged with Miles Sullivan to go on the air with a live show, and that he would, in effect, give further instructions while he was on the air.

He looked up from his desk. Mr. Kubec had been fussing nervously with the controls on his camera. Now the man looked over at him. "Are you sure you know what you're doing, Alvin? No rehearsal, no script, no tape, no instructions, nothing."

Alvin gave him the thumbs-up sign that everything was going to be all right.

The other two cameramen, the electricians, the newsroom crew—everyone was in place, but had no idea what parts they would play in the next few minutes.

Miles Sullivan's voice broke through Alvin's thoughts.

"You may remember that a few weeks ago we put the young newsroom staff of our IBS affiliate in Riverton, Indiana, on the air for some rather unusual treatment of the news, sports, and weather. They have another story for us tonight, of a very special nature. Alvin Fernald has the story."

Mr. Kubec's camera light winked on.

"Good evening, all you newswatchers in TV land," said Alvin. He went straight to the point. "Yes, it's a special story, Miles. And the story's two principal characters are with me in the studio tonight. One is my cameraman, Mr. John Kubec . . ."

There was a startled gasp. Then through his earphone Alvin heard Don Brooks quietly instruct one of the

other cameramen to pan around until he was focused on Mr. Kubec.

"... and the other is my Junior News producer, Peter Hardin." The third camera swung to pick up a startled Pete, seated in a chair at the side of the studio.

"Eleven years ago a bank robbery took place at the First Federal Bank in Santa Maria, California. My associate Scott Lewis in Santa Maria has that part of the story. Over to you, Scott."

Alvin watched the monitor as the network technicians instantly patched in Santa Maria, and Scott Lewis' face filled the screen. He was a strange, intent little man, obviously nervous about his first appearance on network TV. He was standing on a mountain road.

"The story starts on April 18th, 11 years ago. At approximately 8:00 a.m., two gunmen ambushed the guards of a still-empty armored truck on the outskirts of town. They put on the guards' uniforms, and at 9:38 a.m. drove up to these doors of the First Federal Bank."

Alvin watched the monitor. A cameraman more than two thousand miles away picked up the front of the bank, and then moved in toward the doors.

"It was a gray and rainy morning, and very few people were out on the streets. No one noticed anything unusual as the two men entered the bank. Inside, the men disarmed the bank guard, whose name was John Kolsky. They seized a million dollars in small bills. They made their escape in the armored truck that was waiting outside, taking along Kolsky at gunpoint, presumably as a hostage. When Kolsky reappeared later in the day, stating that he had escaped from the gunmen, he was accused of being the inside accomplice who had arranged certain details of the theft. He was convicted of bank robbery, served six years in the penitentiary, and was paroled. He then disappeared. Back to you, Alvin Fernald."

On the air again, Alvin said. "Stand by for your remote pickup, Scott." He paused for a moment, then plunged ahead. "Shortly before the robbery, Kolsky's wife died while giving birth to their only child. The child lived—a boy—and shortly after his conviction Kolsky arranged for the baby to be taken in by a great-aunt and great-uncle who live here in Riverton."

Alvin didn't dare look over at Pete. "That boy is now 11 years old. He's one of my best friends, and the producer of this program. His name is Peter Hardin. Until this moment he has not known that my cameraman John Kubec, alias John Kolsky, is his father."

The air of tension in the studio was almost a physical thing. Alvin looked up. All the blood had drained from Mr. Kubec's face. He took a hesitant, half-stumbling step, then raced toward Peter, leaping over the maze of cables strewn like spaghetti on the studio floor.

Peter leaped to his feet, his chair careening over backward. His eyes were huge. He took two hesitant steps, then hurled himself forward. Two more steps and his face was buried in his father's coat.

Tears streamed down John Kubec's cheeks as he hugged his son tightly, slowly swinging him back and forth as though he wanted to hold him even closer.

Alvin glanced at the monitor in front of his desk. The other two cameramen had picked up the reunion. Don Brooks, up in the control room, was a real pro. He was giving directions to the whole studio crew, through their headsets; the story was being picked up live, and telecast throughout half the world.

Alvin cleared his throat. "Without question, Mr. Kubec was innocent of the bank-robbery charge." He glanced at the monitor. One of the cameramen had swung around, and now the picture of the man and boy locked in each other's arms dissolved, and Alvin's face again appeared on the screen.

"Yes, he was innocent. The two robbers had indeed forced him to go along as a hostage. They drove the armored truck up an unused canyon road. Somewhere along that road, John Kubec leaped from the truck. He rolled down the side of the mountain, and crashed into an orange-colored boulder.

"The armored truck disappeared around a curve. No one has ever seen it since; the two gunmen have never surfaced; and there has been no trace of the loot.

"I know where the loot is. In fact, I know where the truck and gunmen are." He paused, then with an innocent look on his face he peered straight into the camera and asked, "Shall I go on, Miles?"

A low-throated chuckle filled the room. Then Miles Sullivan's voice boomed out. "Alvin, thirty million people are waiting for the end of your story. The entire network is yours. I wouldn't dare take you off the air."

There was a shuffle in the studio. Mr. Kubec came

back to his camera, one arm around Pete's shoulder. Pete was looking up at him, a dazed smile on his face. Mr. Kubec stationed himself behind the camera, and the red light winked on. He's a real pro, too, thought Alvin.

"We knew the truck had to be somewhere up that road. But where? Mr. Kubec had stated to me, unwittingly, that he had counted to 14 after diving from the armored truck, before he found himself smashed against the orange boulder. In order to pin down the point at which he escaped, I had my sportscaster, Shoie Shoemaker, conduct some tests. Here's a tape of Shoie in action."

Obediently the monitor showed Shoie racing down Scheunemann's Hill on his bike. Just as he reached the camera he hurled himself into the air. The bike careened on down the hill. Now, taped in slow motion, Shoie did a lazy somersault, landed on the side of his face with a whoosh, and rolled on down the hill, counting loudly. At the count of "14" he managed to stop. Stumbling to his feet, he pulled out a tape and measured the distance to the point where he had dived from the bicycle. He seemed to be having trouble with his left arm.

The monitor screen went blank.

"Shoie performed that experiment three times, with good results."

Mr. Kubec panned his camera over toward Shoie, who was standing at one side of the set. There was a huge bandage over his left eye and ear, his lower lip was so swollen it hung to one side, and his left arm was in a sling.

"The bandages weren't the good results I was talking about. Shoie rolled an average of 61 feet down the hill while counting steadily to 14. I informed Scott Lewis of this, and he searched the right-hand side of the canyon road. Armed with the 61-foot measurement, he was able to find the precise orange-colored boulder that John Kubec crashed into. Shoie was off by only 18 inches.

"We now have localized the truck into a relatively small area. It must have vanished somewhere between the orange boulder and the getaway car the thieves had left at the top of the canyon, but had never used. How far is it between those two points, Scott?"

"Only about three-quarters of a mile."

"It seemed to me that the weather might play an important part in this mystery, so I asked another member of my newsroom staff, weatherperson Daphne Fernald, to find out what the weather was like on the day of the robbery. What did you turn up, Pest—I mean, Daphne?"

A light winked on another camera, picking up Daphne. She was standing with a pointer in her hand in front of her crayon-streaked map.

It was the Pest's big moment. She was on network television in prime time. "First, I'll throw in a weather forecast free, for all you folks around Riverton." She climbed down from the stool and swung a bare foot up onto it. "My weather toe is sticking straight up in the air, just as fine as can be, and has a warm, snuggly feeling all around it, like just after you step out of a hot bath, so I as Junior News Weatherperson officially proclaim that tomorrow will be warm for this time of year, and with gobs of sun all day.

"Now, Alvin, I checked with that nice Mr. Peabody who is head of all our Weather Service—the Weather Service all of us own, there in Washington—and believe me, folks, we have a real nice man operating our weather here in this country; and Mr. Peabody said that in Santa Maria 11 years ago they had six straight days of heavy rainfall up to and including the day they robbed the bank, which somehow Mr. Kubec got blamed for it which isn't fair. I don't mean he got blamed for the rain, but for robbing the bank."

"That's enough, Daphne."

"Oh, Alvin," she said, still on the air, "I forgot to tell you. Starting next week on our regular newscast here in Riverton I'm going to do an 'advice to the lovelorn' column right on the air, so if any of you viewers out there in videoland are having any trouble with your love life, write me a letter about it. I'll put it right on television and I'll probably solve your problem, too."

"That's enough, Daphne." He paused, then resumed. "It seemed to me that all that rain might have had something to do with the disappearance of the truck. I relied on Scott Lewis to dig up that part of the story. And I mean dig. Over to you, Scott."

The face of Scott Lewis appeared on the monitor, in the mountain setting. "We inspected the stretch of road between the orange boulder and the grove of trees where the getaway car was parked. And we found what you suspected, Alvin. There was convincing evidence that there had been a severe mudslide as a result of all the rain, half a mile up from the boulder. It had even washed out a small part of the road. It seemed reasonable to assume that the heavy armored truck, churning slowly up that road, could have run over a soft spot and actually touched off the mudslide. I'm standing now just above that slide."

Another camera took over. It showed a rutted mountain road. Off to one side of the road was an area bare of any trees, covered only with low scraggly brush. Two big bulldozers crawled at an impossible angle across this slope, working as a team, pushing dirt away from one small area. A huge wrecking truck stood by on the road, its hoist ready for action.

Scott Lewis' voice took over again. "About an hour ago the dozers found something, and they've just about got it uncovered. There goes the wrecker into action now."

Two men pulled a heavy cable, an enormous hook on its end, down the slope, and hooked it to something the camera could not yet see. The wrecker's engine made a low rumble, and the cable pulled taut.

Slowly, out of the dirt and into camera range, crawled a battered, dirt-laden vehicle. The armored truck.

The Magnificent Brain had come through again.

"Good show, old bean!" exclaimed Shoie. Thirty million people heard him say it.

Alvin opened his mouth, microphone ready, then closed it again. Instinct told him the TV screen was telling the story; no words were necessary.

The truck crawled slowly up the slope, pulled by the cable. When it neared the road, a figure scrambled down to meet it. A closeup camera took over. Scott Lewis approached the truck, a remote microphone clipped to his jacket. He reached inside one smashed window, then slowly pulled his hand back out. As the armored truck came to a stop, he walked around to the rear. He rubbed dirt from a small window slit in the back door, and peered in.

"What do you see?" asked Alvin softly.

"One dead man in the cab. Another in the truck. And some bags that must contain a million dollars in small bills."

There was a long moment of silence. Then Alvin's face again appeared on the monitor. "And that's the way your Anchorman, Alvin Fernald, sees it this 12th day of December. Over to you, Miles."

Homecoming

20 As though by instinct, everyone who had been involved in the broadcast gathered at the studio the next morning to celebrate. It was Saturday.

Mr. Kubec, normally quiet, was bubbling with words and laughter. He could not bear to be more than three feet from Pete. And obviously the feeling was mutual. Pete kept looking up at the man with proud and admiring eyes, almost the eyes of ownership. Now he had a father.

Mr. and Mrs. Waters were there too, shy but obviously overjoyed. And they were as proud of Pete as his father was.

At one point Alvin overheard Pete say, "I guess I'm the luckiest kid in the world. I have not just one, or two, but *three* parents." Mrs. Waters hugged him immediately.

The news studio was not in use that time of day, and that's where they gathered. Alvin's parents looked on from the sidelines with proud, if somewhat puzzled, expressions, as though they couldn't understand this strange being who was their son.

Alvin walked over to where Don Brooks was standing with a smile on his face.

"Well, I was wrong, Don," said Alvin.

"Wrong about what?"

"About newscasting being an easy job. I've never worked so hard in my life. And I think it's about time for me to quit the anchorman's job—to leave television."

"I'd hate to see you do that, Alvin. You've done a terrific job of building our ratings."

"Yep. I'm going to quit. I just made up my mind."

"We'll miss you, Alvin. Maybe you kids can make a guest appearance now and then, just to keep our new advertisers happy."

"I'm sure we can do that."

"And I'll bet you'll find something else exciting to do the minute you step out that door, Alvin."

"Anything my mind can imagine, I can do, Don."

The door to the studio swung open, and the blonde lady who worked the switchboard called, "Miles Sullivan is on the phone. He wants to talk with a Mr. Alvin Bernard on closed-circuit television."

Mr. Kubec overheard the message and swung into action. He turned on his camera, and rolled it toward Alvin's desk.

Alvin walked over and sat down. He reached forward and flicked on the monitor, then switched channels to the one that magically locked him into New York, a thousand miles away.

Miles Sullivan's face swam onto the monitor.

"Good morning, Alvin," said that deep, beautiful voice that spoke daily to millions. "I thought I might catch you at the studio. You can't keep a good man away from his work."

"We came in to talk things over, Miles, and maybe to celebrate a little."

"You certainly have something to celebrate. What a story! A real smasheroo! And speaking of smasheroos, I just arranged for Scott Lewis to get a raise in salary for his fine coverage in Santa Maria."

"That was mighty thoughtful of you, Miles."

"And I've arranged a special bonus for you. You certainly earned it."

"I'm afraid I can't accept it, Miles. Sorry."

"Why not?"

"Well, I've decided to give up anchorpersoning. It's beginning to get just a little boring. Sorry, Miles—that sounded like I was putting you down, and Scott Lewis, and Don Brooks, and all the other neat people I've come to know. That's not it. It's just that I can only do one thing for a certain amount of time, and then I have to find something new and exciting."

Miles Sullivan's face was serious. "I can tell from the tone of your voice that you mean it, Alvin. I won't try to change your decision. But we'll miss you. *Really* miss you."

"I'll miss you, too."

"I want you kids to know that you've taught me a lesson. There's a vast, untapped pool of talent in this country—the kids themselves. I'm just thinking off the top of my head now, Alvin, but I'm sure we can come up with some kind of programming for kids that takes advantage of their interests and talents."

"You betcha, Miles. Kids deserve something better than old cartoons and horror shows and reruns of movies on Saturday and Sunday mornings."

"I'd like to fly you to New York for a few days. As a consultant."

"Sounds like fun. Maybe the Pest, and Shoie and Pete could come along. They might have some ideas, too."

"Great. I'll make the arrangements and let you know."

"Good." A pause. "Well, goodbye, Miles."

"Wait. Don't go just yet." The man's famous eyes crinkled. "Well, criminy, as Alvin Fernald would say, I just have so much fun working with you that I don't want to break this up. When I leave here I have to go to a board meeting, and then I have to have lunch with a batch of news executives, and—well—it's much more fun just talking to you. Tell you what. I'll treat for ice cream and cake and pop if you can arrange to send someone out for it."

"Thanks, Miles. We'll appreciate that."

"Oh, and one more thing. That bonus is for a thousand dollars and it's already in the mail, Alvin. There's no way you can refuse it. What are you going to do with it?"

Alvin gazed thoughtfully off into the distance. "Well, I could use it for some bolts and springs I need for my robot. I could buy a whole set of strong magnets."

Suddenly a little piece of lightning ripped across the Magnificent Brain's gray screen.

"I could do those things with it, Miles. But I'm not going to. Do you remember Martha Z., and how she takes care of all kinds of kids who get in trouble? And how nobody knows about her but the kids themselves? Well, Martha Z. is hoping to rent an old house and change it into a temporary home for runaway kids. She says she might be able to straighten more of them out, and get them back with their parents, if she had some time to work with them. But she's too proud to go around asking for money. I think I'll give her the bonus." He paused. "Well, I might keep out just enough to buy *one* spring that I *really* need."

Miles Sullivan gazed at him levelly for a minute. "I hope you do that, Alvin. And, I wish you were *my* son."

"See you in New York, Miles."

"Goodbye, Alvin Fernald, Anchorman."

Alvin walked out the studio door. He was tired. Maybe today, instead of hunting some other kind of excitement, he'd hike up the river and see if he could spot a fox or a groundhog in West Bluffs.

He looked back. Shoie was at his heels with Daphne tagging along just behind. Pete hung back in the doorway.

"Want to come along?" Alvin called to Pete. "Maybe we'll hike up the river."

It didn't take Pete long to make up his mind. As he turned back into the studio, he said, "No. You kids go on. I'm going to help Dad move in. I'm going to help Dad come home."

About the Author

Clifford B. Hicks was born and raised in Marshallton, Iowa, a town much like Riverton, the setting of the Alvin Fernald stories. He began writing professionally as a correspondent for the Des Moines *Register* and *Tribune,* and is the author of several juvenile books and humorous magazine articles. His popular Alvin Fernald series has been translated into three foreign languages, and some of the stories have appeared as specials on "The Wonderful World of Disney." Editor of special publications for *Popular Mechanics* magazine, Mr. Hicks now makes his home in Brevard, North Carolina.

About the Illustrator

Laura Hartman graduated from The High School of Music and Art and from The Cooper Union Art School in New York City. She has worked as a commercial artist and designed handicrafts, kits, and toys before directing her attention to children's book illustration.